"Nancy?" George's voice sounded worried and frightened. "Where are you?"

"You won't believe this," Nancy started to say, when suddenly she heard a sound behind her. As she turned, she was blinded by a flash of light. Then she heard something whoosh through the air above her, and finally something crashed down on her head.

Searing, hot pain exploded through Nancy's brain. Her knees buckled, and someone grabbed the phone from her hand. She heard the sound of the phone snapping closed, breaking the connection with George.

A moan escaped Nancy's lips as she dropped to the floor. She fought to stay conscious in order to focus on her assailant. But as the shadowy figure loomed above her, the room dissolved into blackness and she passed out.

Nancy Drew
Mystery Stories

#79 The Double Horror of Fenley Place
#83 The Case of the Vanishing Veil
#85 The Secret of Shady Glen
#104 The Mystery of the Jade Tiger
#105 The Clue in the Antique Trunk
#108 The Secret of the Tibetan Treasure
#110 The Nutcracker Ballet Mystery
#112 Crime in the Queen's Court
#116 The Case of the Twin Teddy Bears
#117 Mystery on the Menu
#119 The Mystery of the Missing Mascot
#120 The Case of the Floating Crime
#122 The Message in the Haunted Mansion
#123 The Clue on the Silver Screen
#125 The Teen Model Mystery
#126 The Riddle in the Rare Book
#127 The Case of the Dangerous Solution
#128 The Treasure in the Royal Tower
#129 The Baby-sitter Burglaries
#130 The Sign of the Falcon
#132 The Fox Hunt Mystery
#133 The Mystery at the Crystal Palace
#134 The Secret of the Forgotten Cave
#135 The Riddle of the Ruby Gazelle
#136 The Wedding Day Mystery
#137 In Search of the Black Rose

#138 The Legend of the Lost Gold
#139 The Secret of Candlelight Inn
#140 The Door-to-Door Deception
#141 The Wild Cat Crime
#142 The Case of Capital Intrigue
#143 Mystery on Maui
#144 The E-mail Mystery
#145 The Missing Horse Mystery
#146 The Ghost of the Lantern Lady
#147 The Case of the Captured Queen
#148 On the Trail of Trouble
#149 The Clue of the Gold Doubloons
#150 Mystery at Moorsea Manor
#151 The Chocolate-Covered Contest
#152 The Key in the Satin Pocket
#153 Whispers in the Fog
#154 The Legend of the Emerald Lady
#155 The Mystery in Tornado Alley
#156 The Secret in the Stars
#157 The Music Festival Mystery
#158 The Curse of the Black Cat
#159 The Secret of the Fiery Chamber
#160 The Clue on the Crystal Dove
#161 Lost in the Everglades
#162 The Case of the Lost Song
Nancy Drew Ghost Stories

Available from MINSTREL Books

NANCY DREW® 162

THE CASE OF
THE LOST SONG

CAROLYN KEENE

A MINSTREL® BOOK
Published by POCKET BOOKS
New York   London   Toronto   Sydney   Singapore

This book is a work of fiction. Names, characters, places and incidents are products of the author's imagination or are used fictitiously. Any resemblance to actual events or locales or persons living or dead is entirely coincidental.

A MINSTREL PAPERBACK *Original*

A Minstrel Book published by
POCKET BOOKS, a division of Simon & Schuster, Inc.
1230 Avenue of the Americas, New York, NY 10020

ISBN: 0-7434-0688-5

First Minstrel Books printing September 2001

10 9 8 7 6 5 4

NANCY DREW, NANCY DREW MYSTERY STORIES, A MINSTREL BOOK and colophon are registered trademarks of Simon & Schuster, Inc.

For information regarding special discounts for bulk purchases, please contact Simon & Schuster Special Sales at 1-800-456-6798 or business@simonandschuster.com

Cover art by Frank Sofo

Printed in the U.S.A.

Contents

1   Blast from the Past   1
2   Oldies but Goodies   15
3   Double Vision   27
4   Without a Trace   37
5   The Truth Will Out   44
6   Partners in Crime?   53
7   Not So Candid Camera   60
8   A Thief in the House   68
9   Nancy Nabbed   76
10 Pretty as a Picture   81
11 Caught in the Act   92
12 Bad News Blues   107
13 Double Exposure   119
14 A Clever Ruse   133
15 Over the Edge   139

THE CASE OF
THE LOST SONG

1

Blast from the Past

"Nancy! You're drenched!" Bess Marvin wailed one stormy October Friday as her friend Nancy Drew dashed up the steps of the Lakeview University Sports and Recreation Center. A red-and-gold banner, reading Old Can Be Gold, snapped over the entrance in the gusty wind.

Protected from the rain by the portico, Bess had the hood of her pink vinyl raincoat turned down and was fluffing out her straw blond hair. Bess's cousin and Nancy's other best friend, George Fayne, stood beside a large parcel swathed in black plastic trash bags. The three girls had driven to Chicago to check out the antiques and collectibles appraisal show.

Nancy threw back the hood of her slicker and shook out her thick red-blond hair. "My socks may be soaked, but at least this isn't!" The eighteen-year-old produced a blue plastic folder from under her raincoat. Her blue eyes shone with delight as she announced, "My dad's Al Capone Wanted poster is still in perfect condition."

"And the poster's what counts here," Bess declared. "While you were parking, I picked up our admission tickets and a brochure." The corners of several pages were already dog-eared. "There's a guy here who owns Crime Shoppers and Pop Smart. His blurb says he's interested in all sorts of crime memorabilia."

"Let's go for it," Nancy said.

The three friends marched into the state-of-the-art sports facility and lined up to check their coats. A large crowd bearing shopping bags, carryalls, and carefully wrapped bundles milled around the spacious lobby.

Nancy smiled as she glanced at George and Bess in front of her. They were cousins and best friends but so different. Blue-eyed Bess, curvy, fair, and on the short side, was passionate about shopping, clothes, decorating magazines, antiques, and boys—not necessarily in that order. Tall, slim, athletic, with a mop of short dark curls and sparkling brown eyes, George vastly preferred wilderness camping to hanging out at malls.

George bent over and unwrapped her bundle, re-

vealing a rectangular worn brown leatherette suit-
case with metal hardware on the corners. The hardware was dull, rusty, and dented.

"What's that?" Nancy asked as George folded up
the trash bags and stuffed them into her jacket
pocket.

"An old reel-to-reel tape recorder."

"Where'd you find it?" Bess asked.

"Under the eaves in the attic. I bet it's been there
since before we bought the house."

"I hope it didn't get wet," Nancy commented.

"It was all wrapped up. But considering how long
it's been up there, it could be moldy and useless."

"Didn't you bother to see if it works?" Bess
sounded shocked.

"No, actually," George admitted with a sheepish
grin. "I didn't even look for anything to bring until
this morning."

Bess sighed and patted her small pink handbag.
"I only hope Grandma Marvin's Depression-era
bracelet is a treasure. Not that I wouldn't love it
even if it's totally worthless," she added, then
stepped up to the coat check.

Smiling at the girls, the woman behind the
counter took their coats. "Hope you enjoy Old Can
Be Gold," she told them, handing Nancy all three
tags. "Keep your ticket stubs—the admission is
good for the weekend. And we also have a door-

prize drawing every three hours." She checked her watch and made a face. "You missed the last one for today, but starting at ten tomorrow we'll resume the drawings. Prizes are donated by the appraisers and range in value from a couple of bucks up to three hundred dollars. If you like, you can bring your things to those long sorting tables where workers will direct you to the right appraisers. Or you can just browse the show."

"We already know about one appraiser," Bess told her, "so I think we'll head over there."

The girls made their way into the cavernous gymnasium until they were standing in an aisle, staring at a sign: Crime Memorabilia and Pop Culture Treasures.

"I guess this is the place," Nancy said, "though I don't see any appraiser around." As she approached, she saw the table was covered with a green felt cloth. On it she spotted an old fingerprinting kit. The long narrow box was open, its contents protected by an acetate sleeve. Inside the red-and-black checkerboard box was a magnifying glass, a tube of powder, and some papers and other objects. "This must be ancient!" she exclaimed.

"I guess to a girl your age, 1920 seems ancient," a gruff voice interjected. "Hands off unless you want to buy it!"

Annoyed by the speaker's rude tone, Nancy

turned and glared. The man was scruffy and bearded. His hair was salt-and-pepper gray, and he smelled unpleasantly of cigarette smoke. He was only a little taller than Nancy, with a wiry build and muscles that bulged under the sleeves of his black T-shirt.

"I wasn't going to touch it," Nancy said.

"Good," the man snapped.

"Anyway, who are you?" Bess inquired sharply.

"Wes Clarke, proprietor of Crime Shoppers." The man's brusque tone had softened slightly. "You can find me online at CrimeShoppers.com or right here in downtown Chicago." He turned to Nancy. "Sorry to be so suspicious, but in my business . . ." He stroked his beard, then shrugged.

For some reason this guy creeped Nancy out, and she said coolly, "If something's that precious, you should lock it up."

"Oh, the more valuable things *are* locked up, believe me," he snapped right back. "So what are you girls interested in?"

Nancy was tempted to say "nothing" and walk away, but this guy was the only crime specialist at the show. She silently counted to ten, then calmly opened her portfolio. "One of my father's clients gave him this poster some time ago. When I mentioned I was coming here, he suggested I check out the value. You are an appraiser?"

5

"The best in the field around here," the man said, seemingly oblivious to Nancy's chilly tone. He held out his hand. Reluctantly Nancy passed him the poster. It was black and white, and the old paper was yellowed and fraying at the edges. With surprising care Wes removed it from its clear protective sleeve.

He turned it over, held it closer to his eyes, then let out a snort. "Fake," he pronounced, and gave it back to Nancy. "Sorry, but it's not the genuine article. At least a dozen of these turn up at every show."

Nancy frowned. "How can you tell—I mean so quickly?"

Wes Clarke narrowed his eyes. "I *am* an expert. But if you want the details, it's simple. This is computer generated. Nineteen-twenty is pretty ancient when it comes to printing processes. In those days posters were done on presses, with moveable type. This is obviously a photo reproduction."

"But the paper's old," Bess pointed out.

"About a year old, if that," Clarke responded. "It's artificially aged to look old. Believe me, these are pretty good fakes, but they can't fool anyone who knows the first thing about collectibles from the period."

"So it's worthless?" George asked.

"Pretty much. Now, if it were the real thing, it

would be worth quite a bit. Maybe even a thousand bucks."

Nancy inserted the poster in the protective sleeve and put it back in her folder. "I'm half tempted to just toss it," she said.

"Don't do that," Wes said. "It's fun to frame and put up in your room, or wherever. Some folks find the gangster era here in Chicago romantic."

Nancy frowned. The idea of bootleggers gunning one another down ranked far down the list of what Nancy considered romantic.

Clarke didn't seem to notice her distaste. "That's what keeps me in business. The next best thing to knowing how to commit the perfect crime is collecting memorabilia from notorious criminals."

"That's weird," Bess said.

"To each his own," Clarke countered, then his eyes lit on George's tape recorder. "That's probably not worth much either—yet," he told her. "But hold on to it. Another fifty years and it'll be a real collectible. Reel-to-reel machines are going to be as valuable as early nineteenth-century cameras are now." As he spoke, a man with a framed Humphrey Bogart movie poster walked up. The appraiser turned to him, and the girls hurried away.

"Yuck," Bess whispered to Nancy. "That guy was seriously creepy."

Nancy tried to stifle her disappointment. "I hope Dad isn't too let down when I tell him this is a fake."

Next Bess found a Depression-era jewelry appraiser. The woman examined the delicate bracelet Bess had brought. "I'm afraid these stones are only glass, so this probably wouldn't bring more than fifty dollars or so, though it is a very pretty piece. It's a copy of a Diana Toffel design. These red stones would be rubies in a genuine Toffel." Noticing Bess's disappointed face, the woman patted her hand. "But this is still a very nice bracelet."

"Bess Marvin! Is that you?"

Bess turned to her left, where a slender girl with chin-length silky auburn hair was smiling at her. "Lisa?" Bess gasped. "Lisa Perrone—what are you doing here?" Bess reached out and hugged her friend, then noticed Lisa's red Old Can Be Gold T-shirt. "You work for these people?"

"I'm interning for them for the year. It's part of my work-study job here at Lakeview because the arts and antiques program includes learning appraisal work."

"It must be fun," Bess said enviously, then turned quickly to Nancy and George. "This is Lisa Perrone. She worked in that antique clothing store, Threads and Shreds."

"Right before I started college," Lisa said, offering her hand to Nancy and George. Bess introduced her friends.

8

"You're not here just for the day?" Lisa asked. "It's a long trip to have to go back tonight."

"We're staying at a dorm. There was a deal for people who came to the show," Nancy told Lisa.

"You've got to stay with me," Lisa said firmly.

"You have space for all three of us?" George asked.

"I have space for ten of you!" Lisa giggled. "I'm living at my aunt and uncle's condo. I save loads of money, which means I don't have to drop out of school."

"I remember you said that money was tight," Bess commiserated.

"But I've landed on my feet big time," Lisa said. "The apartment is a real palace—on Lake Shore Drive. There are three bedrooms, three baths. Besides, if you guys stay with me, I can show you around a bit."

"You're sure it'll be okay with your aunt and uncle?" Bess asked.

Lisa dismissed Bess's objections with a wave of her hand. "Even if they were here, they wouldn't care. But they're in Malaysia until early next year. I'm apartment sitting, actually. Anyway, tonight there's a really cool party. You guys have to come."

"Far be it from me to pass up a party," Bess said.

"I'm game," George said eagerly.

"Me, too." Nancy grinned. Just the prospect of

9

staying at a comfortable condo rather than in a dorm went a long way toward lifting her spirits.

"Then it's a deal. There's plenty of parking inside the building." Lisa looked at George's tape recorder. "Hey, is that an old tape recorder?" George nodded. "There's a guy who specializes in old appliances. He'd have a good idea what something like this is worth."

"Probably not much," George said.

Lisa shrugged. "You may be right, but, hey, you never know. One person's junk is another person's treasure. I'll walk you over to the table."

Leading the way, Lisa negotiated the crowd, landing the girls at the end of a short line of collectors hugging a variety of old toasters, mixers, and antique telephones. "You're sure this guy knows about tape recorders?" George whispered.

"One of the appraisers here will," Lisa promised. There were several appraisers behind the table, so George's turn came quickly.

"I know this is a bit of a wreck, but you never know," George told the appraiser with a self-deprecating laugh.

The appraiser returned her smile. He was a pleasant-faced man whose suit hung loosely on his thin frame. He saw Lisa, and his smile stretched from ear to ear. "Friends of yours?" he asked.

"Yes," Lisa answered. "This, by the way, is Dave Leinberger," she told the girls, then turned back to

Dave. "I thought this looked kind of unusual." She pointed to the box.

"It does. The carrying case is probably a custom job." The appraiser carefully picked up the case and examined the underside. Then he carefully unsnapped the two metal latches on the front of the case. When he lifted the lid, some of the leatherette crumbled off onto the table.

"It's really in bad shape," George said, but Dave wasn't listening.

"Now, this *is* something unusual," he murmured. "A custom job. This tape recorder is professional quality." He motioned for the girls to gather round. To Nancy's eye the machine looked pretty normal, if old. There was an empty reel on one side of the machine and a spoke to hold a second reel on the other. A row of knobs ran directly below the reels.

Nancy touched a small brass knob on the front of the case. Until the case had been opened, it wasn't visible. "What's that for?"

"Looks like a drawer of some sort," Lisa said.

"Let's see what's inside." Dave eagerly opened it.

The drawer was lined with a faded and moldy velvetlike fabric. A small, flat, black cardboard box was inside. Dave picked it up, and even though he lifted the cover gingerly, the cardboard began to fall apart in his hands. "This hasn't been stored very well," he remarked with a frown.

11

Nancy peered into box and saw a spool of tape. "Do you think anything's on it?" she asked.

"Let's see." Dave met Nancy's eyes and grinned. "This is the fun part." He first put the tape in the machine, then plugged the machine in. A little red light lit up on the console.

"It works!" Lisa gasped.

"Maybe," Dave warned. "I'm not sure the mechanism isn't rusted out." He examined the various knobs, then turned one.

Both spools began to revolve; then suddenly a couple of guys' voices came through the speakers. Nancy couldn't quite make out the words. Something about one last shot at it. Then a voice counted, "And a one, and a two, and a three, and—" Suddenly a familiar gravelly voice began barking a version of a song Nancy knew from somewhere.

"I don't believe this!" George gasped. "That sounds like Lou Knight."

"That's right," Bess said. "But I've never heard that version of 'Dark Side Blues,' have you?" She turned to Nancy.

Nancy shook her head. "It sounds sort of weird. And who's that woman?"

"Carey Black, I bet," a gruff voice announced from behind the girls. Nancy turned and saw Wes Clarke standing there. "And I'd bet more than a pretty penny, Dave Leinberger, that this tape is going to prove pretty valuable—to someone," he added, arching his bushy eyebrows.

Dave eyed Wes cautiously. "You're thinking what I'm thinking," he stated, looking over the heads of the four girls.

"And exactly what *are* you thinking about my tape?" George asked. "It's Lou Knight, and it sounds like a pretty bad version of that song."

"Bad?" Wes snickered. "I wouldn't put it that way. It's unproduced, as in a *missing* jam session, though maybe you girls are too young to know about them."

Nancy gritted her teeth. The man was so condescending she wished she could tell him she knew all about this mysterious jam session, but she had never heard of it.

Fortunately Dave spoke up. "Apparently Knight had jam sessions in his garage back when he was still singing with the Mama's Bad Boys band. Lou briefly owned an old farm south of here. He had a whole recording studio set up in the garage."

"This tape sounds like the one he made with Carey Black, who split from the band right around then, then later resurfaced as a punk rock star," Wes added. "If the tape is genuine, it's worth a fortune."

"You're kidding," George said, paling slightly.

"I'm pretty sure it's the real thing. You'll have to check with a music expert, with better equipment than this recorder," Dave told them. "But if the tape is for real, someone—either a rock music collector or maybe even one of the record companies or the artists—would get into the bidding for it. There might be copyright problems, but you could claim some stake in it since you found it."

"And how much do you think it's worth?" George asked weakly.

"Thousands of dollars!" Wes declared, eyeing the tape greedily.

2

Oldies but Goodies

"Thousands of dollars?" Bess shrieked.

"Not so loud," Lisa cautioned.

Nancy frowned. "Do you have a security problem?"

"I didn't say that!" Lisa corrected sharply.

"The crowd looks nice," Wes said, "but you never know who's casing the joint."

"Oh, Wes, it's not that bad." Dave laughed and turned off the tape. "You make Old Can Be Gold sound like a thieves' paradise."

Wes shrugged. "Yeah, well, better safe than sorry when you've got something that could be stolen easily." He eyeballed the tape longingly, then lifted his shoulders and dropped them. "Well, let me know if it comes on the market." He pulled a card out of his

15

wallet and handed it to George. "Meanwhile I've got to get back to my table. My relief guy will be champing at the bit for his dinner."

As Nancy watched Wes Clarke amble off, someone else caught her eye and she asked, "Why is that guy over there photographing the recorder?"

A tall twenty-something guy was stationed across the aisle, peering directly at Dave's table through the viewfinder of a 35mm camera. He was dressed in a black turtleneck sweater and black jeans, and would have been a standout in any crowd. At the sight of him, Lisa's frown relaxed into a big smile. "Oh, it's just Jason," she told Nancy as she motioned the guy over.

Jason lowered his camera and returned her grin, revealing a pair of adorable dimples. He tossed his straight, longish dark blond hair off his forehead. "Who are your friends?" he asked as he sauntered up. His eyes were a surprisingly dark chocolate brown. As they rested on Nancy, her heart did a little flip-flop. If Nancy didn't already have a boyfriend, she'd definitely be interested.

"This is Jason Woodard, and these are people from home." Lisa introduced him to each girl. "They're in town for the show and crashing at my place for the weekend."

"Then let me get a better shot of all of you, as a souvenir."

Bess interrupted. "We'd love it. Will you send us a copy?"

"Just leave me your address." Jason lifted his camera, and the flash went off.

"So what's the big fuss over here, anyway?" Jason asked, glancing at the tape recorder. "That doesn't look like much."

"Ah, but listen to the tape," Dave said, rewinding the tape and turning the Play knob. "Sound familiar?" he asked.

As the tune played, Jason listened, then shrugged. "It's okay, I guess, but I've never heard it before. You think it's worth something?"

"Could be," Dave said. "Though we need a pop music expert and maybe a soundman to really evaluate it. Meanwhile, George, keep it dry and safe, and don't play it too much. And maybe you should insure it."

"Wouldn't it already be covered under the Faynes' house insurance policy?" Nancy asked as Dave carefully packed the tape back in its original box and put it into the drawer of the carrying case.

Handing the tape recorder back to George, Dave shook his head. "Probably not. Without an appraisal value, the tape would be worth only the replacement value of a reel of blank tape—not very much. You should call your insurance agent—right away, actually."

George made a face. "I guess I can try to reach my parents, but they were going away for the weekend. I don't know anything about their insurance."

Jason cleared his throat. "Don't mean to interrupt, but I've got work to do. I'm off."

"Right," Lisa said, tapping his camera. "Are you going to Low Downs later?"

"What's Low Downs?" Nancy asked.

"A cool blues club. That's where the party I told you about is happening."

"Will you be at the party?" Bess asked Jason.

"Wouldn't miss it—especially if you girls are coming. Do you like to dance?" He directed his smile at Bess.

"More than anything," she flirted right back.

"So, see you then," he said, then headed over to an antique furniture appraiser who had a crowd around his table.

"Where have you been keeping him?" Bess asked, her eyes still glued to Jason's back. "I can't believe you work with a hunk like that."

"I don't. Not exactly. Jason's a freelance photographer," Lisa pointed out. "He specializes in art and antique collections and show catalogs. He's got an impressive clientele and does pretty well. You should see his loft. He owns it, and he's only twenty-two or so."

"So what exactly does he do for Old Can Be Gold?" Nancy asked.

"He works for our publicity department. Last month he was in Denver, and before that, Seattle. He photographs the shows for our publications. He's also available when either an appraiser or one of our clients wants a piece photographed."

"Sounds like interesting work," George commented.

Lisa checked her watch. "Yeah, it is. He loves it. But speaking of work, I've got to get going. I need to be available to troubleshoot any problems. We have another hour or so before we close, so I can meet you at the coat check and then we can head back to my place."

The girls agreed. George got a written appraisal sheet from Dave, and then they set out to find the refreshment area. As soon as they settled down at a table with mugs of hot cider and a plate of chocolate-chip cookies, George asked to borrow Nancy's cell phone. "I'll call my parents now. Maybe they decided to stay home for the weekend after all."

George punched in her number but got the answering machine. She left a message about the tape and also gave her parents Lisa's phone number in case they needed to reach her. "So I guess I can't insure the tape recorder now."

"No big deal," Bess pointed out. "It'll be perfectly safe in Lisa's apartment. If it's a Lake Shore Drive condo, I bet it's got great security."

"And we can deal with insurance on Monday back in River Heights," Nancy added. "Meanwhile we'll hunt down one of those music experts tomorrow, so we can get a more accurate appraisal."

"Now, this is really high tech!" George exclaimed a couple of hours later as the girls stood in the hallway on the twentieth floor of Lisa's apartment building. Lisa punched in a code on the keypad on one side of the front door. "You don't even need a key to get in!"

"Supposedly it makes the place more secure, along with the twenty-four–hour concierge," Lisa said, throwing open the door and flicking on the light switch in the foyer.

"Lisa Perrone!" Bess gasped. "This place is to die for." She plunked down her bag and clasped her hands together.

Nancy had to agree with Bess. The foyer alone was as big as Nancy's bedroom back home. The entrance hall opened into a spacious sunken living room. Most of the far wall was taken up with glass doors, which opened onto a terrace.

"Aunt Betty has a house rule. No shoes inside the house. We change here," Lisa said, pointing to a low bench conveniently located near the door.

As Nancy slipped out of her damp sneakers, she asked, "Does the terrace overlook Lake Michigan?"

"Yes," Lisa answered. "Later, if it clears, we can check out the view. It's beautiful even at night."

Nancy padded into the living room. In spite of its grand scale, the place felt homey and surprisingly cozy. The lighting was mellow, the furniture a wonderful hodgepodge of intriguing Asian chests and side tables, comfortable overstuffed easy chairs, and floor-to-ceiling bookshelves.

"This is really cool!" George exclaimed from across the living room. Nancy joined her in front of a large glass-front case. Inside the case were all sorts of mysterious objects. "Isn't that gizmo some kind of blow dart?" George asked Nancy, putting the tape recorder down beside the curio cabinet.

Nancy nodded. "I've seen pictures of blow darts that look like that." In addition, the cabinet housed an extraordinary collection of knives, carved wooden statues, masks, and small totems. "Where are these things from?" she asked Lisa.

"The dart blowers and knives come from the Amazon, while most of the other pieces are from the South Pacific."

Bess peered over Nancy's shoulder and gave a shudder. "Ugh. This stuff gives me the creeps."

George laughed. "It's probably supposed to. Particularly the masks. Bet they have something to do with evil spirits."

Nancy studied the masks. True, they were a little spooky, but she found them haunting.

The girls picked up their overnight bags and followed Lisa to the back hall, where she showed them to the bedrooms. "Both my room and the guest room each have twin beds." She opened the door to the guest room and showed George and Nancy in. "You guys can share this room, and Bess can sleep in my room, if that's okay with you. I sort of don't like using the master bedroom. Each room has its own bath. Feel free to shower. If you need anything, let me know."

"How dressy is this party?" Bess asked. "We didn't come planning to go to anything too formal."

Lisa shrugged. "It's casual, but if you want to borrow any clothes, I have a closetful, believe me."

Nancy changed quickly into slim black pants, a blue shell, and black jacket. While George pulled on a short black skirt and a deep crimson shirt, Nancy phoned her father, Carson Drew, who was a lawyer. She told him all about George's find and asked him about the legal issues surrounding the tape. He told her that any surviving members of the original band might still have a claim to it, and that since Lou Knight had died in an accident after Mama's Bad Boys broke up, his estate might also have some legal rights to the song, which he wrote. After promising to look into the matter, Mr. Drew told her that Ned Nickerson, Nancy's boyfriend, had called and said she should phone him.

After hanging up on her dad, Nancy dialed Ned at his frat house in Emerson College.

"Hey there, Nan!" Ned's cheerful voice greeted her. "I'm really glad you checked in with your dad. I hope we can hook up this weekend."

"But how?"

"I'm driving up to Chicago tomorrow. One of my buddies at Northwestern University is moving and needs a hand."

Nancy grinned. "Ned, that's great." She then filled him in on what had happened so far.

"I've got another friend in Chicago who's a blues freak. Maybe he can check out the tape to see if it's for real."

"Maybe, Ned, but don't mention it to him yet," Nancy said. "I'm not sure it's smart to have too many people know about it—at least until it's insured and tucked away in a safe place."

"You've got a point," Ned agreed. "But if you change your mind, I can always hook up with him tomorrow night." Then they arranged to meet at Old Can Be Gold late the next afternoon.

A few minutes later the girls left the apartment. "Oops!" Nancy gasped as she began to button her coat in the hall. "I forgot my scarf." Lisa opened the door, and Nancy flipped on the lights, raced back to her bedroom, grabbed her scarf, then hurried to the front door, turning off the lights as she went.

Low Downs, one of Chicago's premier blues clubs, had been closed to the public for the evening so Old Can Be Gold could host a private party for its most important dealers, appraisers, and collectors. At the buffet Nancy and Bess nibbled on a slice of Chicago deep-dish pizza and took in the room. Nancy saw that Lisa was right—this crowd was on the young side.

The atmosphere was lively, and a DJ cranked out music while a live band set up on a small elevated stage.

Lisa joined Nancy and Bess. "I hope you're okay," she said, smoothing her sleeveless cashmere sweater over her short black skirt. "The dancing should be good, and then the live music later will be really out of sight. I'm going to have to mix and be nice to the VIPs here." Lisa wrinkled her nose. "That's the hard part of this job." She nodded toward a slim forty-something man with thinning blond hair, small wire-rimmed glasses, and a well-trimmed mustache. "That's Eddie Landowski. He's my boss."

"Is he the Old Can Be Gold manager?" Bess asked.

Lisa laughed. "More like Old Can Be Gold is his brainchild."

Nancy studied Eddie Landowski. His eyes darted here and there nervously. Why did he seem so uptight at a party? Before she could ask, Lisa was off.

"Look, there he is!" Bess gripped Nancy's arm and made her turn around. "At the bar!"

Nancy obediently followed the direction of Bess's gaze. Sure enough, Jason Woodard was pouring himself a glass of wine. He was wearing the same black turtleneck and black pants he had worn that afternoon. Tonight, however, he didn't have his camera. Nancy wondered why. A party seemed a perfect place to shoot publicity photos.

"Let's go over and talk to him."

"I doubt he'll remember us," Nancy warned.

"I'm not the sort of person who's easy to forget," Bess said blithely.

"That's true!" Nancy conceded—especially the way Bess looked in the black pleather pants and a pale gold metallic top that she'd borrowed from Lisa.

Nancy followed Bess through the crowd as the DJ began a set of Latin dance music.

As dancers took to the floor, Nancy's view of Jason was momentarily obscured. When the crowd parted, she saw he wasn't alone.

He had one hand on the shoulder of a pretty girl with long black hair and big dark eyes. She was about Bess's height, very slim and petite. Bess sighed as Jason steered the girl away from the bar and ducked behind a curtain near the small stage, pulling the girl after him.

Bess sighed again and started to turn away.

Nancy patted her shoulder. "Hey, there are plenty of other great-looking guys at this party, Bess."

"But they aren't Jason," she grumbled, glancing back at the curtain. Nancy rolled her eyes, then watched in surprise as the girl dashed out from behind the curtain. Her face was flushed, and she looked flustered. The girl elbowed her way through the dancers, her eyes blazing, her lips pursed.

"What a creep!" she grumbled to herself as she passed Nancy.

Nancy stared after her. What had Jason done? she wondered, then decided it wasn't her business.

Jason was making his way quickly across the dance floor. He looked angry or annoyed or disgusted—Nancy couldn't quite tell which. Bess didn't seem to notice. She planted herself directly in his path.

"Hi!" Bess greeted him brightly. "Want to dance?"

Jason stared at her as if he'd never laid eyes on her before. His expression darkened. Without so much as a nod of recognition, he marched off through the crowd.

3

Double Vision

"What's his problem?" Nancy shot a look of disgust at Jason's back, then turned to Bess. Bess's lower lip was trembling. The guy had practically reduced Bess to tears.

"Hey, he's just a primo jerk." Nancy patted Bess's shoulder.

Bess heaved a deep sigh, then forced a smile. "Right. Shows you looks can be deceiving. When am I ever going to learn?"

"He had me fooled, too," Nancy was quick to point out. "He seemed so sweet this afternoon." Whatever had happened between him and that girl had put him in a bad mood. Not that that excused him for being so mean to Bess.

"What a two-faced skunk!" Bess gasped, grabbing Nancy's arm.

Nancy followed Bess's gaze. Jason was directly across the floor, talking animatedly to Eddie Landowski and a well-dressed older man. Jason shook the older man's hand, his face all smiles.

Bess snorted. "I guess lowly souls like us don't count."

Nancy shrugged. Privately disappointed, she told Bess, "Jason's probably just working the crowd for contacts, and we shouldn't let him stop us from having a good time." Just then the next song blasted out of the speakers. "I feel like dancing. Come on . . ." Nancy began to tug Bess toward the dance floor.

Bess hung back. "Sorry, Nan. I'm not in the mood. I'm going back to the buffet to drown my sorrows in one of those dips."

While Bess worked her way back to the lavish buffet, Nancy decided to look for George. She skirted the dance floor and pressed herself against the wall. She found herself standing next to the girl Jason had been with.

"Hi," Nancy said.

The young woman turned her dark eyes on Nancy and frowned lightly. "Do I know you?"

Nancy shook her head. "No. I'm here with Lisa Perrone. My friends and I are staying with her for the weekend. You work with Lisa?"

The young woman nodded. Nancy realized that whatever blowup she'd had with Jason, she was over it—or had at least calmed down. "She's our new intern—very nice and smart, too," she said, then smiled. "Oh, by the way, I'm Inez."

Nancy introduced herself and checked Inez's nametag. Her last name was *Rivera*. "So what's your job?"

"I'm a publicist."

"Oh." Hadn't Lisa mentioned that Jason was hired by the publicity department? Maybe his fight with Inez was business related and not a romantic blowup. Curious, Nancy asked casually, "So you know Jason from work?"

"Jason?" Inez repeated neutrally. "You mean Jason Woodard?"

"Yes, the photographer," Nancy answered.

"Sure. I know Jason," Inez said with a shrug. "What about him?"

Nancy was taken aback. Inez was acting as if nothing had happened between them.

"Sorry, got to go," Inez said suddenly. "Some friends of mine just turned up. See you later," Inez closed with a friendly smile, then started toward the front door. Before she took two steps, she stopped. "But if you're looking for Jason, he's over there." She gestured with her head.

Nancy's jaw dropped. Jason certainly *was* right

over there—dancing up a storm with George. The DJ had switched to a hot top-ten swing tune, and George, who adored swing, looked as if she was having the time of her life.

"I don't believe it," Nancy muttered, then noticed that in the very overheated room, Jason had put a red scarf around his neck. His cheeks were bright pink.

The music blared a moment longer, then stopped. George and Jason fell against each other, laughing. George raked back her short hair, caught sight of Nancy, and waved. Grabbing Jason's hand, George practically dragged him toward Nancy.

"Hi, Nancy." Jason grinned broadly.

Nancy was tempted to tell him exactly what she thought of his two-faced behavior.

Before she could, George exclaimed, "Wait until you hear this! Jason has a brother. A *twin* brother."

"Have you seen him around? We look exactly alike," Jason added. "He told me to meet him here." Flashing a particularly warm smile at George, he added, "I sort of got waylaid."

"Did you just get here?" Nancy asked.

"Yeah, probably five minutes ago." Jason hesitated. "Why?"

Nancy giggled softly. "I think I've already met your brother. And Bess and I probably owe him an apology. We wondered why *you* were giving us the cold shoulder, when it wasn't even you."

Jason nodded. "Everyone gets us mixed up, for at least the first three seconds. Then they realize how completely different we are. Ethan's more low-key. I'm the people person, he's more into"—Jason dropped his voice—"he's an antiques geek. He's passionate about everything old or collectible: heirloom quilts, Civil War swords, tribal art, pop star memorabilia . . ." Jason seemed about to say more but cut himself off. "See for yourself," he added.

Nancy saw Jason's double approaching, this time his face wreathed in smiles. The brothers, both dressed in black, were identical. The only clue that they were different men was Jason's red scarf and the fact that his face was still a bit pink from dancing.

Looking directly at Nancy, Jason's twin said, "Hi, I heard you're one of the girls who discovered that Lou Knight tape." His tone was a bit stiff and more formal than Jason's. Nancy couldn't picture him dancing with George. How did a guy like this even *know* who a blues singer like Lou Knight was?

George gaped at Ethan. "Where'd you hear about my tape?"

Before Ethan could answer, Jason introduced him to Nancy and George. Jason added with a wicked gleam in his eye, "Ethan has a way of ferreting out info, don't you, dude?"

31

Ignoring his brother's mocking tone, Ethan shrugged. "I didn't have to dig to find out about the tape. Wes Clarke has spread the word already."

"Why did he do that?" Nancy frowned. "He warned us not to tell people about it."

"I'm sure he didn't tell *everyone*. He knows I'm into pop memorabilia. At the very least I'd love to hear the tape, and if you do decide to auction it, I might put in a bid."

Jason cleared his throat loudly. "As if you could afford it. Or do you have a side job besides the one at Westfield's?"

"I wish!" Ethan said.

"Westfield's?" Nancy was impressed. Westfield's was a small but prestigious fine arts and antiques auction house in Chicago. She'd heard quite a bit about it over the years from her father's wealthy clients. Westfield's had a reputation for honesty and fair dealing. "You work for them?" Nancy's opinion of Ethan went up a notch or two.

Ethan puffed up a little. "Yes," he admitted. "I'm one of two appraisers in training there."

"Translation: entry-level grunt work," Jason teased.

Ethan shot him a cool look. "Someday I'll have a chance to earn commissions—anyway, I do have some savings," he said to George. "Though if this is the lost version of that song, as Wes said, it will be too rich for me. I *am* a bit of a blues freak, and I have every Lou Knight record ever made. I probably couldn't verify that the tape you found is the lost one, but there might be some clues on it about why the band broke up. I'd be interested to check it out."

"I—I don't know." George questioned Nancy with a look.

"The appraiser did say that you shouldn't play it much. It's fragile, and if it broke . . ." Nancy said, shaking her head no.

Ethan hurried to reassure them. "I know lots of professional musicians with professional equipment. The musicians will treat it like gold. And of course you girls would be there. I would never ask you to lend it to me."

"If you put it that way," George said, still hesitant. "But we'll be here only for the weekend."

"That's okay. I can set something up. Are you going to Jason's party tomorrow night?"

"Of course they are," Jason said quickly. "Though I haven't had a chance to invite them yet. Come with Lisa. It's an opening at my loft to show my new prints. Bring your pretty blond friend, too."

"Great," George said.

"And bring the tape with you," Ethan suggested. "I'll make some calls tomorrow to see who has the right equipment."

"Sounds like a plan," Nancy said.

"I'd better run. This is a work night for me," Ethan explained, and started across the floor.

"I'm going to the buffet. You girls want anything?" Jason offered.

Nancy and George both said no. They watched as Jason caught up with Ethan and said something to him.

"Tell me I'm not dreaming!" Bess's exclamation made both girls look around. Bess was staring wide-eyed at the twins' backs.

"You are not dreaming," Nancy said with a smile.

"You're only seeing double," George added.

"There are *two* Jasons?" Bess babbled. Then she started to laugh at herself. "I mean, he's got a twin. Two guys who look like *that*?"

"The other one, the one who really didn't recognize us before," Nancy explained, "is Ethan."

"Oh." Bess paused to digest this. "Still," she said stiffly, "even if he didn't know us, he didn't have to act *so* rude."

"Jason said he's just shy," George said.

"If he's expecting to have a career at an upscale company like Westfield's, he'd better improve his people skills," Nancy pointed out.

A couple of hours later Lisa opened the door to her apartment. "Didn't we turn the lights out?" she asked as they walked into the foyer.

34

The living room wall sconces were lit.

"Nancy came back in for her scarf, remember," Bess recalled. "You probably put the lights on," she told Nancy.

"I did," Nancy admitted with a puzzled frown. "But I'm sure I turned them off again."

"No big deal." Lisa shrugged.

After taking off their shoes, the four girls trooped through the living room on the way to bed. The light switch was near the display case, and Lisa stopped to turn it off.

"Wait!" George gasped, grabbing Lisa's arm. She looked on either side of the glass front cabinet. "Where's my tape recorder? I left it right here, by the case." Panic-stricken, she looked at Nancy. "It's gone!"

So someone *has* been in here since we left! The thought zipped through Nancy's mind. Instinctively she cast her gaze around the room. Nothing seemed out of order. The terrace door was closed. No, she must have just forgotten to turn the lights off. "It can't be gone, George," Nancy said reasonably.

Bess scoffed at the very idea. "You brought it into the bedroom. I'm sure you did. Besides, where would it go?"

Lisa laughed. "It's not like anyone could get into this place."

"Right," George said, hurrying to the guest room. "I probably brought it in here with my knapsack. . . ." Her voice trailed off, and the sound of closets being opened and closed filtered back into the living room.

A minute later a pale-faced George charged out of the bedroom.

"It's not there. Someone's stolen the tape recorder."

4

Without a Trace

Nancy and the other girls gaped at George. After a moment's stunned silence, Lisa spoke up. "George, how could anyone have stolen your tape recorder? No one's broken into this apartment."

Nancy wondered. "Does anyone else know the code to the front door?" she asked.

Lisa replied impatiently. "No. Just me and my aunt and uncle—and the super of the building. I think he has some kind of override code for all the apartments in case of an emergency. The tape recorder has to be in the apartment. George, re-trace your steps. Are you sure you brought it in from the car?"

"Yes, yes," George repeated, annoyed.

"She did. I remember coming up in the elevator

with it. I rested my duffel bag on top of it," Bess said.

"Then you just must have put it down somewhere else, George," Lisa insisted, checking the living room.

"I'll check the bedrooms again," Bess volunteered.

George ran her fingers through her hair. "No. No. I remember putting it down to look at that blow-dart thing in the cabinet. Then I went into the guest room. I'm telling you it's stolen." She sat down heavily on the sofa and heaved a sigh.

Meanwhile Nancy scrutinized the room. She, too, remembered George's leaving the tape recorder by the display case while they checked out the artifacts. Someone had to have been in the apartment after they'd left for the party. And whoever it was had left the lights on.

Nancy checked the terrace door. It was definitely closed. She looked out. The rain had stopped earlier, and now the clouds were breaking up, scuttling across the moon. The lights of Lake Shore Drive sparkled in the waters of Lake Michigan. Nancy wrenched her eyes away from the view and noticed a small puddle of water on the floor by the terrace door. It wasn't much, and it could have blown in under the bottom of the door during the storm.

She touched the door handle. To her surprise, even though a key was in the keyhole, the door slid right open. "Lisa, don't you keep this locked?"

"Why bother? We're on the twentieth floor."

Just then Bess came back into the living room, her expression grim. "George is right, the case has just vanished." Bess sat down next to George, putting a hand on her cousin's shoulder.

Nancy opened the terrace door wider, and a cool breeze streamed in. She queried Lisa. "Okay if I go out here?"

"Sure," Lisa said glumly. "I just can't believe someone stole that tape recorder, George. I feel terrible, and I don't know what to do."

"Call the police for one thing," Nancy suggested, going back to the foyer and grabbing her flats. She went back into the living room and put them on. "I'm taking a look around out here." Nancy ventured onto the terrace, sidestepping the puddles. She looked up and decided that no one could drop down from the terrace above without a rope or some kind of climbing gear. Then she noticed that Lisa's terrace directly joined the one next door. A waist-high metal divider separated them. "Who lives next door?" Nancy called to Lisa.

"No one. Though I think some people may have rented it for a photo shoot."

"Think it's okay if I peek in the window?" Nancy asked.

"Why not? As I said, it's empty."

Nancy climbed over the low wrought-iron divider and peered through the door. She tried the handle. The door was locked. Inside, the apartment was dark, though light from Lake Shore Drive reflected off some metal-shaded lamps. Nancy was also able to make out the vague outlines of a sofa, but that was about all.

Back inside Lisa's apartment Nancy said, "As you said, it's empty and locked. Whoever broke in here came via the terrace, or had the code."

"Is anything else missing?" Bess asked.

"As far as I can tell, no," Lisa said.

"This is totally weird," Nancy mused, looking at the case. "No one even knows if George's tape is real."

"And not many people knew I had it here," George reminded her.

"You can't be sure. If Wes has already told Ethan, who knows how many other people he blabbed to," Bess pointed out.

"Let alone how many people at the show overheard both the appraiser's comments and the tape itself," Nancy reminded them. "We have to call the police," she said to Lisa. "Even if we never find the tape, we'll need a police report in order to file an insurance claim."

Lisa headed for the kitchen. "I'll phone them now."

As Lisa left the room, George said, "Amazing. This morning I thought that tape recorder was a throwaway. Now I'm all worried and upset about losing it."

"And you should be," Bess commiserated. "Trash turns out to be treasure."

"Something doesn't make sense to me," Nancy commented, half to herself. "A thief should have walked out with at least some of the artifacts in that case. I'd better remind Lisa to tell the police about this collection."

She hurried toward the kitchen but stopped at the door. Lisa had her back to Nancy and was speaking softly into the phone. "I'm telling you, they brought that tape recorder here, *with* the tape. Now they've discovered it's missing. What should I do?"

Nancy backed out of the kitchen. Who was Lisa talking to? Certainly not the police. Whoever was on the other end of the line already knew something about the tape recorder. Then Lisa hung up the phone and made another call. "Hello," she said. "I need the police. There's been a burglary."

Nancy walked into the kitchen when Lisa finished.

"I called 911. They put me on hold and said to come to the precinct in the morning to file a report," Lisa said. "I guess burgling an old tape recorder doesn't rank very high on their list of serious crimes."

"In a way they're right," Nancy conceded as George and Bess wandered into the kitchen.

41

"I'm too upset to sleep," Lisa said. "Anyone else want some hot chocolate?"

"Yes!" the three other girls chimed at once.

After making the cocoa, Lisa sat down at the kitchen table and propped her chin in her hands. "This is beyond a bummer, and it isn't the first time this has happened."

Nancy was startled. "You've been burgled here before?"

"No, no. Nothing like that. Believe me, Betty and Nick wouldn't keep the collection here if this building wasn't really secure—at least until now. I'd better e-mail them to let them know what happened, in case they want to move their stuff somewhere safe."

"So then what's happened before?" Bess asked.

"This is really secret—I mean the police know about it—but we're trying to keep it out of the press. Objects that have been appraised at Old Can Be Gold sites around the country have been stolen. No one's been able to pinpoint any connection between the types of things taken, or any of the appraisers at the sites, except that every object stolen was very valuable, say, worth more than ten thousand dollars, or generally of museum quality, or once in a while just highly collectible—like George's tape. It's a real mystery."

Chuckling, Bess turned to Nancy. "I don't mean to laugh, but, Nancy, you've done it again. Headed off for a fun weekend and wound up with the chance to solve a crime."

"What do you mean?" Lisa asked Nancy.

George answered for her friend, "Nancy's got this knack for solving mysteries. It's sort of a hobby with her, except she's extremely good at it."

"I didn't realize that." Lisa looked at Nancy more closely.

"So Nancy can help you and Old Can Be Gold," Bess declared.

"Not so fast," Nancy demurred. "That's up to Lisa's boss. But I am curious about one thing, Lisa. If you knew about these crimes, why didn't you tell us to lock up the tape?"

5

The Truth Will Out

"Yeah, how come?" George chimed in. "Back at the show you told us there was nothing to worry about."

Lisa colored slightly. "Hey, how was I supposed to know this place would be burgled tonight? The security here is excellent, or else my aunt and uncle wouldn't keep their collection in the house."

Nancy felt annoyed. "You still should have warned us that there have been problems related to the appraisal show."

"I couldn't." Lisa's dark eyes were troubled. "It's not like I had any idea that anyone would be after your tape specifically, George, honest. And those other burglaries—they happened after people had received formal appraisals from our experts."

"You should have clued us in," Bess said.

44

"I know. But I couldn't." Lisa blew out her breath. "No point keeping quiet now. Mr. Landowski would have killed me if I mentioned those burglaries to anyone outside of the office. Let alone where someone might have overheard me at the show. It's top secret. Don't you see, if the press and general public finds out about these burglaries, it would wreck our reputation."

"Only if Old Can Be Gold were behind them," George commented.

"Wrong, even the whiff of suspicion that Old Can Be Gold *could* be hooked up with a ring of thieves would close us down," Lisa said bitterly, looking at George. "I'm sorry, but I couldn't say anything."

"That makes sense," Nancy conceded after a moment. "Do you think someone in the company is involved in the thefts?"

Lisa shrugged. She got up and cleared the table of the mugs. "It's a possibility, though whoever it is is certainly good at covering their tracks. And is a real pro . . ."

"Or in league with real pros," Nancy corrected, jumping up to help Lisa. As she sponged off the table, she thought a bit about tonight's burglary. Whoever had broken into the apartment had barely left a trace. The building was so secure, with a twenty-four-hour concierge and secret codes to unlock the doors, that it would take not just skill but some big-time planning to break in. But who would have had time to plan to steal the tape? Nancy tried to focus on possibilities, but she was just too tired.

Bess seemed to read her mind. "I don't know about you guys, but it's past two A.M. and I'm wiped! I'm turning in."

"Me, too," George said, getting up and pushing in her chair. "Let's face it—the tape and the recorder are gone. We probably won't find them again, and I just have to live with it. Besides, maybe they weren't worth much after all," she concluded, forcing a smile.

"That may be true," Nancy said, fighting back a yawn. "But even if someone made off with a perfectly worthless old tape and recorder, they *did* break in here. That's a problem."

"And one you can deal with tomorrow, Nancy Drew," Bess said, putting her hands on Nancy's shoulders and marching her through the foyer. "Everything will look different in the morning."

"Wait, Nancy," Lisa hurried after them. "What Bess said about you being good at solving mysteries, I was thinking—if Mr. Landowski is willing—you might be the perfect solution to our problem. You could investigate the burglaries for Old Can Be Gold, and no one has to know you're doing it, except him, Bess and George, and me."

"That's true. I certainly could keep a low profile."

"So then it's okay if I ask him tomorrow?"

"Your office is open Saturday?" Bess asked, surprised.

Lisa made a face. "Usually, at least mornings. But with the show in town, the whole staff is working overtime, both in the office and at the Lakeview U. gym."

"Then we'll go over together after we file a report on the burglary at the police station," Nancy said.

Lisa brightened. "I'm sure once the boss meets you, he'll be glad to have your help. And, George," she added, "you had better come to the police station with us, since it was your property."

"Right," George agreed. "But I don't think we want to mob your boss at the office."

"No problem," Bess spoke up. "After we finish with the police, George and I can go back to Old Can Be Gold to scope out the scene there. Maybe we'll overhear something about the tape. Word sure seems to travel fast with those appraisers. . . . Take Jason's brother knowing *all* about your even having a tape, George."

"Oh, Ethan knew about it?" Lisa frowned. Then shrugged. "Why am I surprised? The antiques and collectibles scene is a small world, and word spreads faster than fire. Bess has a point. We can all meet up for lunch when Nancy and I get back from the Old Can Be Gold office."

✿   ✿   ✿

Though it was primarily a traveling antiques appraisal show, Old Can Be Gold was headquartered in downtown Chicago. The next morning, when Nancy walked into the office suite located on the fifteenth floor of a deco-era high-rise, she was impressed by the art on the walls, and the Giacometti statue on a pedestal in the reception area. Lisa led the way past the receptionist and, after dumping her bag and jacket in her cubicle, headed directly for her boss's office.

The door was open. Lisa crossed her fingers and mouthed "Wish me luck" to Nancy, then knocked on the doorframe.

"Mr. Landowski, may I come in?" Lisa asked from the doorway of the large corner office.

"Of course. Did that tape recorder ever show up?" he asked, then spotted Nancy and frowned, casting a quizzical look at Lisa. Before proceeding farther into the room, Lisa waited for Nancy to come in, before closing the door.

Nancy looked around. Windows lining two walls revealed a brilliant blue sky. Dark wooden bookcases held elegantly bound books, and a tall grandfather clock in a mahogany case stood in dignified grandeur to one side of the vintage desk. Mr. Landowski was seated in a leather chair behind the desk. Its wooden surface was uncluttered and gleamed with the patina of age.

Lisa cleared her throat, then gave her boss a small nervous smile. "I'd like you to meet my friend Nancy Drew. She was at the house last night when I called you. It was her friend George's tape recorder that was stolen." Mr. Landowski's frown deepened, but Lisa plunged ahead. "I told her all about the other burglaries."

"Lisa, you swore not to mention them to anybody outside of this office," the man said in a shocked voice.

"She explained all that," Nancy said, hurrying to defend the other girl. "You see, Lisa knows I have a knack for solving mysteries. She thought I might be of help to you and Old Can Be Gold, if you want to use me."

Mr. Landowski eyed Nancy skeptically. He folded his arms across his chest and rocked back in his leather desk chair. "Why should you be able to find out more than the police, who have been looking into these burglaries? And why should I trust you?"

Nancy stood taller. "Because I'm honest. My father's Carson Drew—he's a lawyer. Sometimes I help with investigations involving his cases. You can check with him. Often I can find out things that the police can't."

Mr. Landowski studied Nancy from behind his wire-rimmed glasses. "That's probably true," he admitted after a moment. Steepling his fingers, he asked, "How much has Lisa told you?"

Nancy turned to Lisa. "Only that the burglaries keep happening after objects have been appraised at your shows."

"And usually after we've left town," he added. "Though of course we've brought the police in, as have the victims of the burglaries, but we have asked them to keep a very low profile. Some insurance investigators have also been snooping around, trying to ferret out the bad guys, but so far"—he lifted his shoulders in a shrug—"all trails seem to peter out."

"Have they been concentrating on your staff?" Nancy asked.

"Of course, though I'm sure it's not someone on staff, or not on my permanent staff. We do very thorough background checks," he said.

Nancy considered that and made a mental note to learn more about how Old Can Be Gold operated. "Maybe so, but being exposed to all these valuables and the kind of money collectors are willing to pay, even on the black market, can change people."

Mr. Landowski arched his eyebrows. "You're young but pretty smart. I can see that. Okay. Why don't you get on the case. But I'd prefer that no one outside of the office staff know that you're involved."

"Bess and George will have to know, too," Lisa

said. "They're here with Nancy, and it's George whose tape went missing."

"Then that can't be helped," Mr. Landowski said, not looking too happy about Bess and George. "But it's important we don't panic the clientele at the show." He promised to provide Nancy with anything she needed for her investigation, including access to records, data banks, and so forth. "Inez Rivera can help you there. Just let her know you're looking into the other burglaries, without mentioning last night's. . . . After all, we don't absolutely know that it's connected to the others. It could be random."

But probably not, Nancy thought.

The grandfather clock chimed half past the hour. Mr. Landowski capped a fountain pen lying on his desk, then stood up. "I've got to get over to Lakeview now to see how the show is going. I'll see you there soon," he told Lisa as he gathered his things and went to the closet. "And good luck, Nancy," he said, putting on his overcoat. "You're going to need it."

When the girls left his office, Lisa stopped by her desk to check her e-mail. Nancy decided to take the opportunity to look around. The layout of Old Can Be Gold was like most offices Nancy had visited. Small cubicles like Lisa's defined a main work area, which was bordered by several private offices like Mr. Landowski's with window views. As Nancy strolled down the corridor, she saw that most of the private spaces were empty. Most but not all. A small corner office was lit, the door ajar.

Nancy cautiously peered inside and smiled. "Inez?" she called out, recognizing the young woman in front of the computer screen. The screen was covered with data and some photos. Nancy couldn't make them out from her vantage point.

Inez's head snapped up. "What are you doing here?" she gasped, then with a quick gesture punched her keyboard, blanking out the screen.

6

Partners in Crime?

What does Inez have to hide? Nancy wondered, but she masked her interest with an apologetic smile. "Didn't mean to interrupt your work. Lisa's showing me around the office, and I saw that your door was open."

Inez relaxed a little. "Sorry to be so jumpy. I was shopping, and we're not supposed to go online for personal stuff from these computers," she said, lowering her voice to a conspiratorial tone.

What a lame excuse, Nancy thought. "So, that party was pretty hot last night," Nancy said, changing the subject as she moved into the room. "I'm Nancy, in case you forgot."

"Uh, right. You were looking for Jason?" Inez stood up, putting her hands in the pocket of her hooded sweatshirt. Like Nancy, she was wearing jeans. It was obvious to Nancy that Inez was trying to block her view of the desk. From where Nancy stood, all she could see was a stack of five-by-seven index cards near the computer. "Did you find him?"

"Yeah, I did. I met his brother Ethan, too."

Inez didn't react to Ethan's name. "Always weird seeing the two of them together" was all she said. After a moment's hesitation, she asked, "How long have you known Jason?"

"I met him yesterday," Nancy said. "He was photographing people at one of the tables at the show. He said he works for the publicity department, which I guess means you."

"In a way, I guess he does. I give him assignments, clue him in on who's brought items of interest to the show." Inez gestured absently toward the stack of cards.

"Oh, you keep track of who's brought what to the various shows?"

"Of course. We build a client list for ourselves to notify people where we'll be next."

Nancy filed that information away. Probably all of the burglary victims had home addresses in the Old Can Be Gold database. That could be evidence that someone in-house was involved.

Something didn't jibe, though. "My friends and I

all had objects appraised yesterday," Nancy said, "but we didn't fill out cards. How come?"

"Sometimes items that aren't worth much fall through the cracks. An appraiser figures that you won't be return business. What did you have appraised?"

Nancy told Inez about the fake Al Capone Wanted poster and Bess's jewelry. She decided to mention George's tape recorder since there was a good chance Inez knew about it anyway. "And my friend has this funky old reel-to-reel tape recorder," Nancy said, deliberately not mentioning that it had gone missing.

"I heard," Inez revealed readily. "Wes Clarke was saying it might be a real find because of a lost song on a tape inside the machine."

"No one bothered to have George fill out a card, either." The more Nancy thought about it, that meant that whoever burgled Lisa's apartment not only didn't need to know where George lived, but somehow knew about the girls' last-minute decision to stay at the condo. To Inez she added, "Was that some sort of oversight?"

"Dave would be equipped to judge the machine but probably not the tape. Whoever he referred your friend to would have her fill out a card when she brings the machine in today."

The more Inez talked the more certain Nancy was that she knew nothing about the burglary the night before. She *had* been acting suspicious when Nancy walked in. Maybe what she was doing on the computer was against company rules but not related to the thefts.

Nancy decided to pick her brain some more. "Don't you guys worry that something might get stolen at the shows?"

"Stolen?" Inez paled slightly. After a moment she asked, "Have we ever been robbed?" She shot Nancy a piercing glance, as if trying to read her mind. "No, we haven't had any incidents outside of the occasional pickpocket reports. Even those are pretty rare. Old Can Be Gold prides itself on being safe for collectors."

"Oh, Inez," Lisa spoke up as she entered Inez's office. "You don't have to lie to Nancy. She knows all about the burglaries, and she's going to help us find out who's behind them."

Inez looked abruptly from Lisa to Nancy. "I don't understand."

Nancy was sure Lisa's revelation had made Inez more nervous, so Nancy tried to reassure her. "Mr. Landowski has asked me to look into the burglaries."

"So that's why you were quizzing me." The defensive tone in Inez's voice was unmistakable.

"Nancy was quizzing *you*?" Lisa looked sharply at Nancy. "Inez didn't have anything to do with those burglaries."

Nancy threw her hands up and managed to laugh. "I didn't say she did. I just wanted to find out what kind of records you guys kept of your clients."

"Well, I would have felt better if you had been upfront and just asked me about the databases," Inez informed Nancy tightly. "But I'm glad you're on the case, and I wish you luck in cracking it."

Inez sounded sincere enough, Nancy reflected as she and Lisa left the office. But at the same time Nancy believed that Inez was hiding something—whether it was related to the burglaries, Nancy had no idea.

All she knew so far was that the robbery had occurred while the girls were at the party and that whoever had broken into the apartment knew that George had brought the tape there. Had someone trailed them to the building and sneaked past the concierge? Nancy visualized the hallway. The apartment was down a side hall, out of sight from the elevators. Could someone have watched Lisa punch in the code last night? Nancy couldn't imagine how the girls would have missed someone in the hall. Nancy made a mental note to find out if there were other ways to steal a keypad code. Once inside, the thief could have locked the door behind him or her and left via the terrace and . . . and what?

As she drove to the university, Nancy reminded herself she should check the terrace again by daylight. Somehow in the morning rush she had forgotten. An agile cat burglar could manage a getaway scaling up the terraces to the roof. The scenario was improbable but couldn't be ruled out.

Still, Nancy's experience had taught her that the simpler a theory, the more likely it was right.

Nancy wondered if Lisa should be put on her list of suspects. Lisa could have given someone her apartment code—or lied about someone else's already having it. Nancy hated suspecting Lisa, but she had to be checked out.

Who else knew where they were staying? Nancy tried to recall who had been hanging around the appraisal table. Dave Leinberger of course. Then there was that weird Wes Clarke. Why had he even bothered following them to the table? Nancy wondered as she exited the highway. Wes had *said* the recorder was probably worth less than peanuts. Then there was Jason, but Nancy dismissed him quickly. He hadn't even recognized the band.

Suddenly she realized that Lisa hadn't said a word during the whole trip. "Is everything okay?" Nancy asked, shooting a quick glance across the front seat of the Mustang.

Lisa bit her lip, then blurted, "No. No, it's not. I can't believe you made Inez feel like a criminal. She's a friend of mine, Nancy, and she's an honest person. No way she's involved in these burglaries."

"I'm sorry she felt that way, Lisa. But to solve this I have to question everyone. She gave me some good information about the company's databases. Whoever robbed those clients' houses must have had access to the Old Can Be Gold records. If it makes you feel better, I'm pretty sure she didn't know anything about George's missing tape."

Lisa looked at Nancy hard. "You thought she had something to do with that, too? That's crazy—besides she was at the party with us."

Then, before Nancy could frame a response, Lisa grumbled, "Next thing you'll tell me is that *I'm* a suspect, too."

7

Not So Candid Camera

"Lisa, I never said you were a suspect!" Nancy cried, truly dismayed. Could the girl read minds or what? Sure, she couldn't rule Lisa out, but Lisa wasn't high on Nancy's suspect list.

"No, you didn't," Lisa admitted. Pushing her hair off her face, she regarded Nancy with a hurt look. "But it sort of makes me uncomfortable knowing you're investigating *everyone* at Old Can Be Gold. We're all friends and colleagues."

Nancy hurried to reassure Lisa. "I'm just trying to do my job, and I have to ask lots of questions. Sometimes," Nancy added gently, "that makes people uncomfortable."

Embarrassed, Lisa laughed. "I guess so. Criminal investigations are pretty new to me."

When she reached the university, Nancy parked in the area at the back of the gym cordoned off for Old Can Be Gold employees. The rear of the building was equipped with freight loading docks. A corrugated metal gate was up, revealing the cargo area.

As they climbed out of the car, the wind scuttled leaves across storm puddles from the day before. "Is this where they bring the larger pieces into the show?" Nancy asked.

"Exactly," Lisa replied. "We can go in this way, with my employee pass."

The two girls jogged up the short flight of concrete steps leading to the loading dock. Large wooden crates, sturdy moving boxes, and some intriguing-looking trunks with Old Can Be Gold lettering on the sides were haphazardly stashed around the area.

Lisa made her way through the forest of containers and stopped at the security desk. The guard scrutinized Lisa's ID, then let her in. At least security on the back end of the show is pretty tight, Nancy thought.

"I can see why nothing goes missing from the shows themselves," Nancy said as Lisa led the way through a large room that was functioning as a warehouse. "Tell me," Nancy asked as they headed into a hall, "have any of the burgled items been large—like pieces of furniture or paintings?"

"I honestly don't know the details of the burglaries, though I did overhear about the latest one, in

Seattle. A woman's collection of art deco jewelry went missing. That's pretty portable."

When Nancy and Lisa reached the main appraisal area, they were greeted by the pleasant but loud hubbub of the crowd. "Mr. Landowski wants me to work behind one of those large triage tables by the entrance, so I'll leave you now," Lisa said. "When did you say Ned was coming around?"

"Ned!" Nancy exclaimed. "In all the commotion I practically forgot we're meeting here later. Probably not until four or so, depending on how his friend's move goes. I told him to look for us at the food court."

"Sounds good to me," Lisa said. "But wait for me, in case I get tied up." As she left, Lisa called over her shoulder. "And don't forget, Ned's welcome to come to Jason's party."

A few minutes later Nancy found George on the edge of a small crowd looking with interest at a pair of infant-size moccasins. An appraiser was talking about the unusual beadwork. Midway through the little lecture George caught Nancy's eye and motioned Nancy aside.

"Those were beautiful," Nancy remarked as they moved out of earshot. "Did you guys turn anything up? And where's Bess?"

George chuckled. "Bess is in love. She latched on to Jason Woodard the minute she spotted him. To find Bess, look for Jason. But as for turning up any

clues regarding my missing tape recorder..."
George made a thumbs-down sign. "I canvassed this whole place. There aren't many pop-culture people at this show. They all seemed to know *all* about the tape, thanks to that creepo Wes Clarke."

"Did they know about the robbery?" Nancy asked.

George shook her head vigorously. "Didn't seem that way. They seemed to know only that a tape exists. One music specialist told a client that he heard that a valuable seventies blues/rock tape was about to come on the market, and he sent the client over to Wes. So then I kind of snooped at a table behind Wes's. Sure enough, Wes was bragging about how he could put his hands on a really rare Mama's Bad Boys tape, for a price."

Nancy grew thoughtful. "I can't say I like Wes, George, but that's not proof he knows that the tape was stolen or where it is now. He'll probably make you an offer as soon as he hears you've had it appraised. But just in case he does know about the burglary and is involved, I'll feel him out now." Nancy turned to go, but George stopped her.

"Look, Nan, there's Bess!"

Bess was posing jauntily beside an antique cigar store wooden Indian while Jason snapped her picture. As soon as the shutter clicked, Bess waved Nancy over. She looked particularly pretty, with her cheeks glowing and her baby blue eyes bright.

"She's head-over-heels already," George murmured.

"More like Jason's been nabbed," Nancy whispered as they approached.

"Hi, guys, look who I found!" Bess hooked her arm through Jason's. He patted her hand, then extricated himself and went to talk to a heavyset mustached man.

"If you want, I can send you a picture of your statue after the show closes," Jason said as he handed the man his card.

"Are you sure you can't have it here tomorrow?" the man asked, wistfully looking at the wooden statue. "I do have a buyer in mind, and he might pick it up at my house on Monday. I'd like to have the photo in hand before I sell the piece. It's been in my family for several generations."

Jason made a face. "I won't have time to process this roll by the time you leave, but if you give me your home address and phone number, I'll overnight it to you on Monday. You'll have it Tuesday first thing."

"It's a deal!" The man wrote Jason a check to cover the cost of the photo, then gave him a card with his address.

"I should get a picture, too." Bess pouted prettily.

Jason laughed and hooked her hand back through his arm. "It's a deal. I'll leave it with Lisa.

She's in touch with you guys, right? And she told me she's going back to River Heights next weekend."

When Jason didn't ask for Bess's address, her face momentarily registered disappointment.

"Uh, George, sorry to hear about your missing tape," Jason said abruptly.

"How did you find out about—" George started to say, then shot a scathing glance at Bess, who just smiled back.

"Come off it, guys," she said. "You can't be worried about Jason. Since he makes the rounds of all the appraisers he might hear gossip and help us."

"I had no idea you were a detective," Jason said, carefully appraising Nancy. "So Landowski is going to let you work for him?"

Nancy sighed, then returned Jason's smile. "I guess he is."

"Good," Jason said. "New blood will help get to the bottom of all those burglaries. The cops sure have hit a dead end."

"You know about the burglaries—I mean besides last night's?" Nancy was surprised. Jason was not a staff employee of Old Can Be Gold.

Jason rolled his eyes. "Of course I know. It's supposed to be top secret, but word gets around. Anyway, good luck," he wished Nancy as his name was called over the P.A. system. "See you tonight. Don't forget the party."

As soon as Jason had left, George turned on Bess. "How could you, Bess? No one's supposed to know Nancy's on this case, and we definitely were keeping last night's burglary under wraps."

"Come off it, George. It's no big deal," Bess protested. "It's not like Jason's a suspect or anything."

"You can't rule him out," George fumed.

Bess giggled. "Of course you can. He was at the party with us last night during the break-in."

"So was Lisa," Nancy said. "I haven't ruled her out, either."

Bess just gaped at Nancy. "You're kidding, right?"

Nancy shook her head. "I'm not. At this point anyone with access to that apartment or to company records is a suspect."

Bess glared at Nancy. "Lisa is a friend of mine, and you have no right to accuse her."

Lowering her voice to just above a whisper, Nancy explained, "I'm not accusing her of anything, but she could have set up the thieves—though why, I'm not sure."

Bess blew out her breath. "Money," she said reluctantly. "Remember Lisa mentioned what a break it was that her aunt and uncle let her live in their condo this year? Last night she told me that she almost had to drop out of school this year. Her dad was laid off, and now her parents don't have to pay rent, at least for this semester."

66

"So the tape recorder could be tempting," Nancy mused.

George didn't look convinced. "I think she was genuinely surprised that it was stolen, Nancy."

"And she had no way of knowing George was bringing it to the show. Did she even have time to contact anyone and tell them it would be in her apartment last night?" Bess asked, sounding hopeful.

"That's been bothering me, too," Nancy admitted, though Lisa hadn't been with them between when George's tape recorder was appraised and when they all left together for the condo. Also, Nancy recalled, she had lost track of Lisa at the party. Obviously she couldn't have left the party, but she could have made a call, either yesterday afternoon or last night, to an accomplice or accomplices.

"Nancy, there you are!" a man's voice called out. Nancy turned to see Eddie Landowski plunging through the crowd toward her. His thin face was creased with worry.

When he reached her side, he said in an urgent soft voice, "We need to talk now! *Alone!*"

While George steered Bess toward a display of porcelain figurines, Mr. Landowski took Nancy aside. "It's happened again, this time in Denver," he bleated woefully. "A priceless Tiffany lamp is missing."

8

A Thief in the House

"Someone is targeting our clients!" Mr. Landowski exclaimed, clearly distraught. "We can't keep this under wraps much longer. Once word gets out, Old Can Be Gold will be dead in the water."

"Did the police give you any details?" Nancy asked, trying to divert his attention away from publicity problems.

Landowski nodded. "Yes, but they told me the report they just faxed to the office showed nothing unusual, except that this time there was a good deal of vandalism to the owner's house." He frowned. "Could that mean this is a different gang of thieves?"

Nancy couldn't be sure, but she doubted it. Checking out the police report might help, so she asked if she could see it.

Landowski agreed readily. "I have to make a cou-

ple of calls, though—quench the fires, so to speak,"
he told her.

"One more quick question," Nancy said as he
started back toward his small temporary office. "Do
you know anyone who might *want* Old Can Be Gold
to go out of business? We've assumed the thieves
are only interested in stealing high-ticket items. Another motive might be to hurt your organization."

Mr. Landowski looked startled. "No one that I
can think of, but I suppose it could be a motive."

Not the most likely one, Nancy mused as Mr.
Landowski left, but something to keep in mind.
What bothered Nancy was the timing of the theft of
George's tape recorder. Why had it happened during the show and not after the show had left town,
and after George had brought it back home? Was
this burglary just a coincidence and not connected
to the others?

And without Lisa's help, how could anyone have
gotten into that apartment? Then a thought struck
Nancy. She hadn't talked either to the concierge or
the superintendent of the building. Nancy checked
her watch. It was too late to drive all the way back to
the condo and return in time to meet Ned. There
was enough time, though, to pay another visit to
Wes Clarke.

"What was *that* all about?" George asked, inter-
cepting her en route.

"Was there another burglary?" Bess piped up.

"That's what I just heard," Lisa added, joining them. "Word's out among the staff. It's a real bummer. That couple with the lamp back in Denver were nice folks, too."

"You go on the road with the company?" This was news to Nancy.

Lisa nodded. "Yes. This semester, as I told you, is all work-study. I don't have any formal course work here, though I have to write a couple of papers on my experiences. I travel to most of the cities. Let's see . . ." She paused to think, then ticked off the cities on her fingers. "I was in Dubuque, Fargo, Boise, Seattle, and then in Denver."

"Doesn't give you much time to enjoy that condo," George remarked.

"Believe me, I'm here enough to have gotten used to the luxury. And life on the road is fun, but I don't have to do it long enough for it to get old. Now, take Jason—he says he gets tired of the travel."

"Jason travels with the show, too?" Bess asked.

"Sure. Not everywhere, although we were in Denver and Seattle together—I guess it depends on his other freelance assignments. I suspect that for all his playboy image, Jason's a bit of a homebody. His hobby seems to be decorating his loft. It's appeared in *City Home Design.*"

Bess's eyes widened. "Are you serious?" When

Lisa nodded, Bess clasped her hands together and sighed. "I cannot wait to see the loft."

"Speaking of Jason's loft," Lisa said, "it turns out I can't go back home with you guys before Jason's party." She dug in her bag, pulled out an invitation, and handed it to Nancy. "I have to stay here until closing time. Ethan or someone will give me a ride. I'll meet you guys there. Fortunately I have a change of clothes here."

"But *we* need to change," Nancy pointed out, wanting the opportunity to check out the condo, the staff, and the apartment next door. "Can we go back without you?"

"Sure," Lisa said. "I'll have to give you the code after I swore I'd never give it to anyone. For the record this is a first." She jotted the numbers on a piece of paper and handed it to Nancy.

"I'll tear it up once we're inside," Nancy promised lightly, safely tucking the paper into her purse.

"See ya later." Lisa waved goodbye.

"I'm starved," Bess complained. "We missed lunch. Can we eat while we wait for Ned?"

"I'm sort of famished, too," George admitted.

Nancy was hungry, but she wanted to talk to Wes Clarke before leaving the show. She also needed to find Ethan to learn about seventies pop-culture collectors. With luck she might also be able to psych out his relationship with Inez. The young woman's suspicious behavior at the office had sent up a red flag. Was Inez's little scene with Ethan the night before about something personal, or was it connected to the missing tape and the burglaries?

"You guys head over to the food court," Nancy told Bess and George. "If Ned turns up early, tell him I'll join you in ten or fifteen minutes." Nancy checked her watch, then took off for CrimeShoppers.

As Nancy approached CrimeShoppers, she saw Jason, camera in hand, meandering down the aisle behind Wes's table. Jason caught her eye, winked, and mouthed, "See you at the party!"

Nancy grinned back and continued toward CrimeShoppers, where Wes was huddled next to another man—a collector or potential customer, Nancy figured. Gesturing animatedly as he talked, Wes had his customer spellbound.

Nancy slowed her pace and quickly reconnoitered the area. At the table next to Wes's, a small crowd was bunched up close to an appraiser who was carefully examining the bottom of a blue-and-white Chinese vase. Positioning herself behind one of the onlookers and out of Wes's line of sight, Nancy strained to overhear his conversation.

The general din in the room drowned out all but a few words. Nancy caught something about "could be highly collectible" and a "record producer." But before she could hear more, the woman in front of her moved, and Nancy found herself directly in front of Wes.

"Oh, hi!" he said, startled to see her. He quickly shoved something under his counter. Before he did, Nancy saw the object was a thin square cardboard box—the kind that could hold a reel-to-reel tape. He slapped his customer's shoulder. "Come back later," he told the man. "I might know more then. Meanwhile . . ." Wes put his finger to his lips.

The man nodded. "Right. I know the rules, Wes." The man checked his watch and frowned. "I have to leave now. How about I come back tomorrow?"

"Fine, fine!" Wes said, giving a meaningful glance at the shelf beneath the table. "I'll be here."

As the man strolled away, Wes directed his attention back to Nancy. "So," he said, rubbing his hands together, "you did come back." He looked past Nancy into the crowd. "Where are your friends?"

Nancy gave a casual shrug. "The food court, at the moment."

"What did your friend find out about her tape?" Wes asked.

"Nothing yet," Nancy said, dying to see what was in the box Wes had stashed under his table. "Actually, I was going to ask you what *you* came up with."

"What do you mean?"

Nancy detected a defensive note in Wes's voice. With a sweet smile she lifted a finger and made a playfully scolding gesture. "You certainly have spread the word that such a tape exists. By now I figured you would have checked out its worth."

"What makes you say that I spread the word?" Wes's expression shifted. There was definitely a gleam of respect in his small hazel eyes now. Nancy felt as if she were his opponent in some kind of game, except Nancy wasn't sure what the game was about. Was Wes daring her to come right out and accuse him? Was Wes involved with the ring of thieves targeting Old Can Be Gold's clients? Or was he still just trying to ferret out information about the tape's value?

Nancy continued to play dumb about the robbery. "Last night at Low Downs, Ethan said you told him *all* about the tape."

"All that I knew *then*," Wes corrected her.

"And that was?"

Wes frowned. For a minute he appeared genuinely puzzled. He finally gave a small shrug. "Nothing more than we knew about it yesterday—how it could possibly be a recording of Lou Knight's last song."

Nancy regarded Wes carefully. "Come off it, Wes," she said, adopting a playful tone. "You told us yesterday to keep quiet about the tape, not to publicize its existence until we were sure what it was. Then you go and tell Ethan—and who knows who else?"

Wes shook his head. "Sure I mentioned it to a collector or two, and then to a couple of guys in the music biz, who frankly said they'd give their right arms for it, but there was no harm in that. Your friend will probably be talking to some of the same guys today, if she hasn't already. Wait . . ." Wes narrowed his eyes. "She's already gotten a firm appraisal and is looking for bidders, isn't she?"

Before Nancy could respond, some kind of ruckus erupted behind her, the crowd pressed around her, and she was bumped from behind, nearly careening into Wes's arms.

"Hey, watch it!" someone yelled at the table behind them. Nancy and Wes both turned in protest.

"What's going on?" Wes shouted.

"I don't know," the appraiser at the next table replied. "I almost dropped this vase, and it's very valuable," she added. "It's getting too crowded in here." The woman carefully handed the vase back to its owner.

"I don't believe this!" Wes's bellow made Nancy jump.

"What happened?" she asked.

"I've just been robbed!" he roared, his hand closing on Nancy's wrist like a vise.

9

Nancy Nabbed

"Let go of me!" Nancy demanded, wriggling free of Wes Clarke's grasp.

Wes ignored Nancy's protest. He pointed at the shelf behind Nancy. "Look, it's gone. Did you see anyone lurking around here?"

"No, I didn't." She peered at his display shelf. At first she didn't notice anything out of place. "What's missing?"

"The fingerprinting kit you were looking at yesterday," he said, a funny expression crossing his face. He narrowed his eyes at Nancy, then shook his head. "I had my back turned," Wes grumbled, "but you were facing the shelf. Did you see anything?"

"No, I didn't," Nancy replied, "but are you sure you had the kit out today?"

Wes rolled his eyes. "Of course I'm sure." Then he muttered, "Whoever pilfered the kit purposely caused a disturbance in the crowd, then, when our backs were turned, stole it. Well, I'd better go get Security."

"Do you want me to watch the table until you get back?" Nancy volunteered. She wanted a chance to look under the table to check the box Wes had been so quick to hide.

"No, no." Wes brushed her off. "My friend Derek is used to covering for me." He motioned toward a nearby table where a tall gray-haired man was sorting vintage comic books. "Could you mind the shop a minute? I've just been robbed and want to find Security."

"Sure," Derek said. "That's a first at one of these shows," he commented.

"Guess there's a first time for everything," Wes said sourly.

"Do you want me to come with you?" Nancy asked.

"You said you didn't see anything, so there's no point. But where will you be in case Security wants to talk to you?"

"I'm heading to the food court, to meet up with friends, but I might stop at Westfield's first," Nancy told him.

Now, Nancy thought, she would never get a

chance to get a close-up look at that box . . . not un-less she came back after hours or early tomorrow.

"Nancy, right?"

Nancy looked up into the chocolaty brown eyes of one of the Woodard twins—but which one?

Then she noticed that he wasn't carrying a cam-era. "Ethan?"

"You're good!" Ethan beamed. "Most people can't figure us out so fast. You seem to be a very figuring-out sort of person."

"You're kidding, right?" Hadn't Jason told his brother that Nancy was investigating the burglaries?

"About what—about my being Ethan? No. I *am* Ethan. What was the giveaway?" he asked, seem-ingly oblivious to Nancy's mocking tone.

Nancy decided to play along and take Ethan at face value. "No camera!" Then she realized that wasn't the only difference between the twins. Ethan's general demeanor was a bit more snobbish than his brother's.

"So are we still on for tonight?"

"Uh, sure, at Jason's party."

"That, too. But I meant about listening to your friend's tape afterward. My musician friend has recording equipment at a club not far from Jason's digs."

Nancy couldn't believe her ears. Had Jason really kept quiet and not even told his own brother? Or was Ethan playing dumb?

"I can't wait to hear it!" he said enthusiastically. "I mentioned it to a couple of rock historians, and they said that it could be worth a pretty bundle."

Nancy stared at Ethan. His enthusiasm set off alarms in her mind. If Ethan was involved in the theft, that might explain why last night's burglary didn't match the others. Still, since Ethan had been at the party, he needed a partner in crime—someone with the know-how to break into Lisa's apartment.

What about Inez—was there any chance Inez and Ethan's blowout was related to the robbery? Maybe both Inez and Ethan were involved. Before Nancy could mention it, the gymnasium speakers crackled to life.

"It's now time for the second door-prize drawing of the day. The holder of ticket number 23928 is the lucky winner."

A woman behind Nancy shrieked, "I won. I won!" A cheer went up from the vicinity of the winner. Then Jason's voice rose above the general din. "Step back, step back, everyone. Let me get the lucky lady's photo."

Jason backed right into Nancy, knocking her carryall out of her hand. Everything spilled out.

"Whoops! Sorry—oh, it's you, Nancy!" Jason apologized. "Let me help you pick up your stuff."

"Take your picture," Nancy said, waving him off. "This is no big deal."

"Look! I knew it all along—that girl's a shop-lifter!" Wes's voice accused as someone gripped the back of Nancy's arm and yanked her to her feet. She found herself looking into the stern face of a security guard. Beside the guard, Wes stood glaring at Nancy.

Wrenching his eyes from her face, Wes bent down and picked up Nancy's notebook, a blue print scarf, her car keys, and one last item—a familiar red-and-black box. Nancy instantly recognized it as Wes's missing fingerprinting kit!

10

Pretty as a Picture

Stunned, Nancy couldn't find her voice. She stared at the fingerprinting kit in disbelief. How had it landed in her bag?

Nancy had no time to figure that out just then. She faced the guard squarely and declared, "Look, there's some kind of mistake here."

"I'd say so—a pretty big one," Wes sneered. "Yours!"

"You'd better come with me—quietly," the security guard urged Nancy. "We don't want to make a scene, do we?"

Nancy could have laughed out loud. Wes had shouted his accusations loudly enough to be heard clear out to the parking lot. Drawn by the commotion, a curious crowd was already clogging the aisle.

Nancy ignored the gentle pressure of the guard's hand on her elbow and refused to budge. "I did *not* steal that kit from CrimeShoppers. I don't know who did, but whoever it was must have planted it in my bag."

Wes scoffed. "Sure, and the moon is made of green cheese."

"What's going on here?" George cried, elbowing her way to the front of the crowd. Relief swept over Nancy at the sight of her friend. Right behind George was Bess, and behind Bess, a familiar tall, dark-haired figure.

"Ned!" At the sight of her boyfriend, Nancy could have cheered.

"Nancy?" he gasped, staring first at Nancy and then at the security guard. "What do you think you're doing?" Ned asked the guard angrily. "Let her go now!"

"Look, mister, you stay out of this. This girl was caught red-handed with stolen property."

"Stolen property?" Bess shrieked. "Are you guys nuts? Tell them, Jason. Tell them about Nancy."

"Look, blondie, stay out of this," Wes commanded.

"Wes," Jason broke in. "I'm sure there's some mistake."

"Tell him Mr. Landowski will vouch for me," Nancy urged Jason.

"I'll try to find him," Jason said, turning to go.

"I'll page him," the guard said. "Though just because the girl knows him doesn't prove she's not a thief." As the guard punched a number in his pager, Ned sidled up to Nancy and squeezed her hand.

"What's going on here?" he asked softly.

"A lot's happened since last night. I'll fill you in later," she murmured. "Here's Mr. Landowski now."

Eddie Landowski was pushing his way through the crowd. "What is going on here, Hugo?" he asked the guard angrily. Then he spotted Nancy and his eyes widened. "Nancy, what happened?"

Before Nancy could open her mouth, Wes answered. "She was caught red-handed with goods she shoplifted from my table."

"That's crazy." Mr. Landowski dismissed Wes's charge with a wave of his hand. "Nancy is no shoplifter. She's working for me. . . ."

Nancy winced, inwardly begging him not to blow her cover.

"Under cover, because some small items have gone missing, and I wanted her to check out shoplifters."

"Man, no one told me about this." The guard looked annoyed.

Mr. Landowski said curtly, "Well, now you know."

Wes looked disgruntled. "Look, Mr. Landowski, how do you explain *this* in her bag?" He showed Mr. Landowski the fingerprinting kit.

"Maybe a real shoplifter planted it," George suggested.

"My thought exactly," Mr. Landowski said. "Are all the parts still there?" he asked Wes.

Wes nodded reluctantly. "You're not going to let her get away with this?" he fumed.

Mr. Landowski held firm. "I'm sure this has to do with her ongoing investigation."

As the crowd dispersed, Nancy motioned for Ned, George, and Bess to wait up. "I've got to talk to Mr. Landowski alone, but then let's head back to the condo. You can follow us," she told Ned.

"I don't have a car. We drove up from Emerson in Russ's car. They dropped me off here to meet you."

"So we'll all leave together then." Nancy dug in her purse for her coat check and handed it to George. "Why don't you get the coats, and I'll catch up with you by the front entrance."

When her friends left, Nancy pulled Mr. Landowski aside.

"How *did* that kit get into your bag? I know you didn't steal it," Mr. Landowski said.

"Beats me," Nancy said, feeling angry and used. "It's a good bet that whoever planted it is onto me."

"Do you have any leads?" Landowski asked, pushing up his glasses.

Nancy shrugged. "Yes and no. I have a couple of

suspects. But the clues are still too vague to put together. I'll update you later or tomorrow."

"Just keep me posted," Eddie Landowski told her. "I don't like the idea that someone is on to you. Things could get dangerous."

Driving back to Lisa's condo, Nancy caught Ned up on events.

"Your theory that whoever wants you off the case planted Wes's kit in your bag makes sense," Ned said. "Any prime suspect?"

Nancy slowly shook her head. "Not really. Just strong possibilities."

Propping her arms on the back of the front seat, George leaned forward. "When would someone have had a chance to put that kit into your bag?"

The commotion at the porcelain appraisal table had given any thief the perfect opportunity to steal something, Nancy decided. "There was one chance when I was at Wes's table. And another when I was talking to Ethan a little later."

"So Wes was around," Bess pointed out.

Nancy nodded. "And who's to say he didn't plant the kit when he brought the guard over. He picked it up off the floor—not Jason."

"Jason was there, too?" George remarked.

"Come to think of it, Jason had two chances to plant the kit. I saw him near Wes's table before this commotion started in the crowd. And he was snapping pictures right before I dropped my bag." Nancy paused. "I think he knocked into me."

"Not Jason," Bess huffed. "No way. Though I wouldn't put it past his snobby brother."

"Who, by the way," Nancy informed everyone, "still thinks he's going to hear the tape tonight."

"You didn't tell him it was stolen?" George asked.

"More to the point, *Jason* didn't tell him," Nancy observed.

"Now, that's hard to believe," George said. "If I had a twin, I'd let him in on the fact that the tape he was so interested in was lost."

Ned shrugged. "Maybe. But just because they're twins doesn't mean they get along."

"Good point, Ned," Nancy said. "I'm not sure if they *do* get along, but I get the feeling that they aren't very close."

"So Ethan might or might not have known about the theft," Bess said. "But if he did, then he should be a suspect."

"Believe me, Bess, I haven't ruled anybody out at this point," Nancy said, pulling into the underground garage at Lisa's condo.

"What gets me," Ned said as they climbed out of the car, "is that the other items stolen are so different from the tape."

"Part of me thinks the theft of George's tape is just coincidental," Nancy admitted as they waited for the elevator. She handed Bess the paper with the code to Lisa's apartment. "I've got to check out a couple of things with the staff here. Why don't you guys get changed. I'll be up in a few minutes."

Nancy jogged up a flight of stairs to the basement level and found the super repairing a screen in his workshop. She introduced herself as a friend of Lisa's.

"Did you hear about the burglary last night?" she asked.

"What burglary?" he said in a heavy Russian accent. "I cannot believe an apartment in this building is robbed. This place is like—what is the name of that place with all the money in it?"

"Fort Knox," Nancy supplied. "I hate to tell you this, but whoever broke in didn't have any trouble accessing Lisa's apartment."

"You mean apartment Twenty H?"

"Yes," Nancy said. "Do you know who has access to the door?"

"You mean the code?" The super shook his head. "No one, unless the girl or her relatives gave it to someone. Sometimes people do give the code to someone, to water plants when they are away, or in case they forget it."

"How do you get in if there's a plumbing problem, or if some other emergency comes up when no one's home?"

The super's smile faded. "You think I do this? All the time people think because I come from another country I am not honest. You police?" His eyes narrowed with suspicion.

"No," Nancy said quickly. "I'm not the police, and I'm not accusing you of anything. I just need to know if there's any other way into the apartment, or if someone can use your code."

The super shook his head vehemently. "To go into apartment if there is emergency, I use special code, like you say, and I need to have another employee of building with me. Also I have to let management know by phone that I am accessing apartment."

So the building security was tight, much as Nancy suspected. Nancy thanked the man and headed up to talk to the doorman. She remembered she hadn't asked the super who had rented the apartment next door to Lisa's. Well, the doorman might know, she told herself.

What luck, Nancy thought as she approached the tall, uniformed man leaning on the concierge's desk, reading his newspaper. The same guy as the night before was on duty.

He seemed to recognize her instantly. "Ms. Perrone's friend," he said as she approached the desk.

Good, Nancy thought, he remembers faces.

Nancy glanced at his nametag. "Carl," she said, "I don't know if Lisa told you, but last night something was stolen from her apartment."

Carl seemed amazed. "Last night? When? The police never came on my shift."

Nancy made a face. "No, and they aren't coming over. What went missing sort of falls into the category of petty theft, and I guess they have more serious crimes to investigate."

"I hope you filed a report at least," Carl told her.

"We did. But I wondered if you noticed anything suspicious last night—or late yesterday afternoon when we came in. Did anyone you didn't recognize follow us upstairs?"

Carl shook his head instantly. "No—why?" He paused. "You think someone saw her punch the door code?"

"Could be," Nancy admitted.

"I can't swear no one was lurking anywhere in the building—I'm not at the desk every minute. When I take breaks, I lock the front door."

Nancy walked over to the entrance. The building had two sets of doors. An outside door led to the elegantly landscaped drive that led to the front of the building. Just inside the door was a panel of buzzers. If the doorman closed the second set of doors, a tenant would have to buzz any guest in. "So when you're not here, people have to be buzzed in."

"Yessss . . ." Carl sighed deeply. "Unfortunately sometimes tenants have buzzed in strangers—in spite of the security camera that is tied in to each apartment. Next to the intercom system is a little TV screen where a tenant can see who the visitor is."

"And people still buzz in perfect strangers?" Nancy was amazed.

"It *has* happened, though I don't know that there have been any robberies as a result. The worst thing that's come out of it was some vandalism in the garage."

"But someone could have unknowingly buzzed the thief in?"

"Yeah," Carl conceded, "but how they'd crack the door code is beyond me."

Nancy started toward the elevator, when she remembered. "Carl, one last thing. You know the apartment next to Lisa's—is it still vacant? She says someone sublet it recently."

"Um—yes." Carl's tone became guarded. "A photographer rented it—short term—like for a couple of days," he added quickly. "Don't know much about it, though. You might ask the weekday guy." Carl rushed to open the door for a tenant.

Nancy continued to the elevator. Why was Carl uncomfortable talking about that sublet?

Upstairs, she asked Ned. He had found his way to the kitchen and was microwaving popcorn. "Hey, in buildings like this there's a good chance he's getting a little something under the table to let the guy use the apartment," Ned told Nancy. "Maybe it's not a real sublet."

Nancy nodded. "That would make sense—and I bet the super's in on it, too. Though if not, that means Carl knows the code to that apartment."

"And you're thinking that he might know the code to this one, too—that somehow Lisa's relatives had given it to him." Nancy remembered the super had mentioned that people sometimes gave codes to neighbors, just as in a traditional building you gave a neighbor a key.

"Could be."

"Oh, Ned," Nancy complained. "Now I have to add Carl to my list of suspects. He might have helped someone have access to the apartment next door. I wish I could check it out somehow—unfortunately, that terrace door is locked, unlike Lisa's."

"Maybe you could break—"

A terrible scream went up from the back bedroom, cutting off Ned's next words.

11

Caught in the Act

"Bess!" Nancy cried, rushing into Lisa's bedroom, Ned and George right on her heels. Bess was standing in the open doorway to Lisa's closet. Her face was pale, but otherwise she looked okay. Nancy's heart stopped racing. "What happened?" she asked, touching Bess's arm.

"You look like you've seen a ghost!" George exclaimed.

"Look," Bess said in a tragic voice. She turned and pointed into the spacious closet. Nancy walked in. It boasted a custom-made system of drawers, shelves for sweaters, cubbyholes for shoes, and separate hanging areas for short and long clothes. An acoustic guitar case was propped against the back wall. The top drawer of a built-in unit was open.

Planted squarely in the middle of a stack of scarves was a reel of tape.

"The tape!" Nancy gasped, not wanting to believe her eyes.

George pushed past Bess. "Lisa had it all along!"

"Oh, how could she?" Bess wailed.

"Where's the box?" Nancy asked, picking up the tape and rummaging through the scarves.

"And the tape recorder?" Ned added, taking the tape from Nancy and looking it over.

"She obviously ditched it," George grumbled as Ned brought the tape out of the closet.

"Are you sure this is the right tape?" Ned's skeptical tone made Nancy look up. "I'm no expert, but this tape doesn't look thirty years old to me."

Nancy took it back and examined it again. "I can't swear it's the same tape, Ned, but it sure looks like the one Dave Leinberger played yesterday."

"I'll check the closet for the recorder," George volunteered, and plunged back in. "It's not here," she said a minute later.

"But where is it, George?" Nancy wondered. "If Lisa is the culprit, then there was no break-in. But when would she have stolen the tape and gotten rid of the recorder?"

"Beats me," George said. "Maybe she got rid of the box and recorder while Bess was in the shower."

"Got rid of them where?" Bess asked.

"I bet there's a room for trash disposal on this floor," Ned said. "Maybe the recorder is still there."

Ned went to check, then came back empty-handed. "It's not there. So next step is to scare up a recorder so we can play the tape to see if it's really George's."

"I'm sure it is," Bess said. "I mean, why would Lisa have a tape she couldn't even play?"

"More like, why would she hide it?" George said, irritated.

"So where do we find a machine?" Nancy wondered.

"That's easy," George said. "I'm supposed to bring the tape to the party tonight to have Ethan's buddy check it out."

"Maybe we should leave Ethan out of this," Ned suggested. "But I've got a friend who might help us out."

"Who?" Nancy wondered.

"One of my frat brothers' dads owns a blues club here in Chicago. He can probably scare up the right equipment on pretty short notice."

"That would work," George said. "We can go now."

"No," Nancy contradicted. "Not now. Ned, call him, and tell him we'll come over later. I want to go to that party first."

"To confront Lisa?" George asked.

"No, not until we hear the tape. And, Bess, don't

tell Lisa *or* Jason we found it. Remember, we're not a hundred percent sure this is the missing tape."

"I hate that Lisa's the bad guy here, but at least you're getting closer to solving the puzzle," George said.

"I wonder," Nancy mused aloud. "Lisa's stealing the tape doesn't prove that she was involved in the other burglaries."

"Now, why do I get the feeling you don't quite believe Lisa's guilty?" Ned teased lightly.

"Because my gut instincts tell me she isn't. And Lisa wasn't anywhere near me when the finger-printing kit was taken." Nancy checked her watch. "Let's get ready for the party. An art opening should be the perfect place to nose around."

"What a scene!" Ned remarked as he, Nancy, and George lingered near the front door of Jason's loft, waiting for Bess to return from the rest room. The place was wall-to-wall bodies. Outfits ranged from almost formal, to extremely casual, to outrageous— but always stylish.

To freshen up their outfits, Nancy and George had traded pieces. George was wearing Nancy's black trousers, while Nancy was wearing George's miniskirt.

"No wonder this place was featured in a design magazine," Bess commented as she joined them.

"You won't believe his collection of vintage photos. I spotted two Edward Weston prints on the wall. This guy must be loaded."

"Maybe his family has money," Ned suggested, hands in the pockets of his dark cords as he surveyed the room.

Nancy had no idea, but she remembered Jason's teasing Ethan about his not making much money at his Westfield's job. Obviously, Jason was the more successful of the two brothers. Still, Nancy hadn't expected to find such an expensive art collection or such a sumptuously catered affair.

Exactly how did Jason manage to support his expensive tastes? Fencing museum-quality collectibles would be a tempting option. Now that Nancy thought of it, Jason's business contacts—like Lisa's, Inez's, and Wes's—might provide just the right connections.

Putting aside her frustration, Nancy said, "Why don't we split up. George, you feel Ethan out about the tape."

"He expects me to have it with me," George said, "but I'll pretend I forgot it."

"Good thinking," Nancy said. "Bess, why don't you keep Jason occupied. See if you can hang out with him. Ask him about his art—whatever."

Bess smiled broadly. Looking around, she said, "I might have trouble getting close to him, though. Oh, by the way, I saw Lisa on my way back from the rest room. You'll be proud of me. I just said hi." Bess appeared troubled for a moment, but then she brightened. "But, hey, hanging with Jason's not bad."

"What about me?" Ned asked playfully. "Don't I get to help?"

Nancy grinned. "Mingle. Be the social soul you are. Keep an eye on the people Lisa talks to. That might give us a lead."

"So you don't think she was working alone?"

"Not if she's involved in the other burglaries. But if it's just the tape she's stolen, then she's a dead end."

"Which I think would make you happy," Ned predicted.

"Right. I doubt George would press charges once she had the tape back. Without the tape, the recorder isn't worth anything."

As Ned strolled off in search of Lisa, Nancy worked her way through the crush, heading toward Jason's exhibit.

"Nancy!" Lisa grabbed Nancy's arm. She took in Nancy's outfit and grinned. "So you made it home okay. I'm so sorry to have stranded you guys."

Nancy managed a small smile. How could Lisa play so innocent? She was half tempted to confront her, but Lisa wasn't going to give her time to get a word in edgewise.

Lisa rolled her eyes. "This turns out to be an all-work, no-play party for me, though Ethan said something about getting together later—with George, whatever. Anyway I've got to socialize."

"Right."

"Oh, and I heard about your run-in with Wes today." Lisa pursed her lips. "Mr. L. said that Wes was accusing you of stealing. What a creep that guy can be—Wes, I mean."

"That got cleared up," Nancy assured Lisa, although both times Nancy had seen Wes at the party, he'd glared at her. It was obvious he still thought she was some kind of crook.

Before Lisa left, she handed Nancy an envelope. "Mr. L. told me to give this to you. It's that list of burglaries you asked for."

Wondering how Lisa managed to act so innocent, Nancy finally made it to the exhibit. The framed photos were displayed on a whitewashed brick wall. Few people were actually looking at the art. Nancy had no trouble getting close enough to study the pictures.

Unlike Jason's tightly composed colorful commercial work, these photos were all black and white. One group consisted of close-ups of graffiti-covered walls. Nancy moved to the next group and found herself drawn to a haunting photograph of . . . Nancy wasn't sure which twin until she read the title: "My Brother, My Keeper." "Ethan," she murmured, amazed at the brooding photo. Ethan was sitting in a small, simply furnished room. Bookshelves on either side of his easy chair were crammed. The room—and Ethan—were in stark contrast to Jason and his elegant digs. The only items of value in the photo were five or six rock posters on the wall: Nancy recognized one as being from the first USA tour of the Beatles, back in the 1960s. If the poster was the real thing, Ethan must have paid a lot to acquire it.

"The series is called 'How the Other Half Lives.'"

Nancy looked up. Jason or Ethan? The guy was wearing a charcoal gray shirt, a black tie, and a black blazer. He was offering her a glass of something sparkling.

"Just seltzer—you look underage."

Nancy took the drink and sipped it, glad for the cold refreshment. The room, in spite of the cool evening, was hot.

"He means me, of course," the twin said, taking a sip of wine.

"Oh, Ethan, hi!" Nancy wondered why the two brothers were dressed alike. The brief glimpse she'd had of Jason earlier revealed that he was dressed in black and gray as well. "These photos are pretty incredible."

"He's good, you know. I can't deny that. What does bug me is he might get famous for these pictures someday—and they are, after all, a kind of put-down of me. Jason is always mocking my lifestyle."

"Which is?" Nancy probed, taking another gulp of seltzer.

"Minimal." Ethan laughed. "I can't afford any of this. How Jason does is beyond me, but, hey, he's the guy who charged two dollars a glass for lemonade *and* sold out faster than any kid on the block. He's got a talent for money, I guess. Anyway, I'm the family dork. I'd rather work at a low-paying job doing what I love—and one that leaves me time to pursue my real passion."

"I thought appraising antiques was your passion."

"Don't get me wrong," Ethan went on. "I adore antiques and the amazing things people have collected over the years. Every piece has a history— fascinating stories. Usually just family stories, but sometimes you find something George Washington might have handled."

Nancy had to stifle a yawn. "So then what else are you passionate about?"

"Music. Seventies rock music specifically. I'm working on a history of the era. I've already got quite a good discography—you know, a list of all the releases in each given year."

"You're writing a history of seventies rock?"

"You bet. And I might even have a publisher

soon. I met an agent at one of these parties, and he's trying to interest *Tumbleweed* in taking it on. My hook is to have a Web site for the book where, for a small fee, readers can download bits of songs mentioned in the text."

Tumbleweed was a leading rock magazine that had started a book-publishing business, part of which was on the Internet. Nancy would have been impressed, except she was too busy trying to fit in this new piece of the puzzle. Ethan's motive for wanting George's tape was strong. Except it was Lisa who had it. Were they in cahoots?

"What's your relationship to Lisa?" Nancy asked.

Ethan blinked. "Why?"

"Just wondered," Nancy said with a coy smile. "One of my friends sort of likes you but wasn't sure if you were taken."

Ethan returned Nancy's steady gaze. "She's a friend. Though I can't say I'm free right now." Ethan looked over Nancy's shoulder and frowned. "Speaking of friends, one of mine just turned up."

"Wait." As Nancy turned to stop Ethan, she saw Inez hovering by the front door. Nancy caught her eye, and for a second Inez looked distressed; then she flashed Nancy a tiny smile. Nancy quickly said to Ethan, "I was wondering, in this picture"—she pointed to "My Brother, My Keeper"—"there's a Beatles poster on the wall. Is it the real thing?"

Ethan's eyebrows shot up. "What do *you* think?"

"That you couldn't afford it," Nancy said bluntly.

"I couldn't, but I did. Just as I'd come up with the money for your pal's tape." Then he strode away.

Nancy tried to keep an eye on Ethan, but she quickly lost sight of both him and Inez in the crowd. She turned back to the pictures. One a little farther down the wall caught her attention. Like "My Brother, My Keeper," it was black and white. This time the model was a woman: a slim, leggy blond in a clingy black cocktail dress. The model was posed in front of a double glass door. The sky was twilit, and the model was turned away from the camera, so that Nancy could see only the chiseled profile of her face. She looked familiar. In fact, the whole picture reminded Nancy of something. But what?

Nancy turned away and saw Ethan, or was it Jason, bearing down on her. "So are you impressed or what?" he asked with a cocky smile.

Then she noticed the Rolex watch on his wrist. "Jason?"

He put an arm around her. "What if I said no?"

"You'd be lying," Nancy said with more confidence than she felt. "I was just speaking with Ethan about your picture of him."

"And he was less than enthusiastic? Don't deny it."

Nancy evaded the question to press one of her own. "So why *do* you dress alike?"

"We're twins. It's fun. But it's not like we call each other and plan what to wear. I like fooling people, and I know Ethan's wardrobe is limited. He has only one art-opening outfit. Ethan, unlike me, is very predictable."

Nancy filed that information away. "So tell me about *this* picture." She tapped the glass-framed photo with her fingernail.

"What about it?"

"I feel like I've seen it before."

"How could you?" Jason gasped, then quickly regained his composure. "Sorry, didn't mean to react like that. It's just I'm very protective of my work . . . but I know why it's familiar."

Nancy just lifted her eyebrows.

"It's the model. She's Yvonne Bly. She was on last month's *Trend.*"

"Oh, that's it then." Nancy was disappointed. Yvonne Bly was one of the world's top fashion models. "I didn't realize you knew her."

Jason looked smug. "She's a friend. She would have been here tonight, but she left yesterday—or the day before," he corrected himself quickly. "For Paris."

"Jason! Stop hiding. This *is* your party. Your pretty friend has to share you with the rest of us," a large woman said as she walked up. She wore a sequined blouse with a plunging neckline, and an ankle-length velvet skirt. She was middle-aged but very pretty and perfectly made up. She hooked a plump hand through Jason's arm. "I'll bring him back to you later, sweetie, but I want Jason to meet the head of a Taipei gallery. He's in town just for the evening."

Before heading for the rest room, Nancy cast one last glance at the photograph. The title was simply "By Dark of Night." Something about the picture bothered Nancy. Maybe it was the fact that she hadn't recognized the model. Nancy got in line for the guest bathroom. While she was waiting, she noticed the entrance to Jason's work area. He had partitioned off a small room in the back of the loft. In one corner was a door marked Darkroom. One wall was covered with windows, opening out onto a fire escape. In front of the windows was a long desk, and on the desk were a single lamp, which was lit, a computer, a scanner, some photographic equipment, and a stack of photos.

Nancy walked into the room. She stared at the top photo and smiled. In spite of his party-boy image, Jason was obviously a hard worker. He had already developed the photo she'd seen him take earlier that day, the one with the man in front of his wooden cigar-store Indian statue. Nancy realized

Jason must have a pretty good color darkroom to be able to get such professional results. That was his business, though she reminded herself, and he had the money for top equipment.

She cast a quick glance over her shoulder. No one was watching, and it still wasn't her turn for the bathroom. She picked up the top picture. The next one showed Bess and the man and the Indian. Bess looked terrific, though Jason, in spite of his flirting, had done a good job capturing the Indian, catching it at an angle that partially cut off Bess.

She began thumbing through the stack of prints. There was one of George and her and Bess the day before, and right dead center was the tape recorder. Nancy turned the photo over and frowned. Scribbled in a photographic pen was a note: "Knight? Carey? Tape."

Nancy flipped to the next picture, and her frown deepened. It was a picture of a young woman, grinning broadly as she held up a large, elaborate art deco brooch toward the camera. Nancy turned that photo over: just a street address was penned on the back. The next picture in the pile was of a plump grandmotherly woman in a pair of shorts and sandals standing next to a wonderful Tiffany stained-glass lamp. On the other side of the lamp was an elderly man, probably her husband. Nancy slowly turned the photo over and her hand flew to her mouth as she read, "Tiffany/777 Canyon Drive/ Denver."

"What do you think you're doing?" a furious voice cried behind her.

Nancy spun to face the door. Jason was staring daggers at her—or was it Ethan?

12

Bad News Blues

"Messing with stuff on my brother's desk is a real no-no. Believe me, I learned that a long time ago."

Ethan, not Jason. Relief swept across Nancy.

"I wasn't messing around," Nancy protested, then tried to look sheepish. "I really like your brother's work, and while I was waiting for the bathroom, I just peeked at his desk."

Ethan eyed Nancy quizzically. "Why do I get the feeling you weren't just casually checking over his stuff."

His tone was curious, a little mocking, but not angry. Nancy took courage and added, "Well, I wasn't being completely casual. He took some photos of my friend Bess today, and I was looking to see if he'd developed them."

"And . . . ?"

"He has." Nancy grabbed the photo of Bess off the desk.

"Oh, your blond friend," Ethan remarked. "Nice shot. But then, what would you expect from Jason? He's a pro." He leaned over Nancy's shoulder and checked the photos. Nancy wondered if he was trying to see if she'd taken any. Suddenly he chuckled. "I remember this picture. Those folks in Denver with that lamp. It was one of those great Old Can Be Gold moments. What they thought was a copy turned out to be a genuine Tiffany. Jason caught their expressions well."

"You sound as though you were there," Nancy said.

"I was." Seeing the expression on Nancy's face, he laughed. "Don't look so surprised. Westfield's loves the publicity and contacts Old Can Be Gold provides. Why do you think most of the auction and appraisal houses pay for tables at these shows? Primo networking. Westfield's sends me when there's no affiliated appraiser in the area."

Nancy groaned inwardly. So Ethan had as much opportunity as Jason did to scout out the valuable items when the show was on the road.

Ethan flicked out the desk light and closed the door behind them. "Jason would not be happy if more people wandered into his study."

"I'm sure Jason will be glad you were looking out for him."

Ethan winked at Nancy. "Mum's the word. My brother thinks you girls are pretty cool. I don't want to disappoint him. And speaking of cool, I just spoke with George. It's too bad she zoned out and forgot to bring the tape."

Nancy managed a casual shrug. "Well, I guess she'll just have to have it checked out tomorrow at the show or back home in River Heights." Just then a woman came out of the rest room. Fortunately Nancy was next in line, which made it easy to cut short her conversation with Ethan. "See you later," Nancy told him.

Once inside, she took out her notebook and ran her finger down the list of stolen items Mr. Landowski had mentioned. Her suspicions were confirmed: three of the stolen pieces matched photos of items she had seen in Jason's office.

Next Nancy checked the inventory of the robberies Lisa had given her. She wondered how many of the photos in Jason's study matched the stolen items on the list. She was tempted to slip back into the study, but that would be risky. She didn't relish breaking and entering, but she needed to investigate here when Jason wasn't around—maybe tomorrow afternoon when he'd be at the show.

After putting away her notebook, Nancy left the bathroom to search for Inez. Maybe she'd have more luck tonight drawing the woman out. As she made her way through the crowd, Ned appeared at her elbow, ready to head outside. "Nan, I think we'd better leave. I told my friend we'd bring the tape over around eleven, when he'd be between sets. Bess went to get her coat."

Nancy hesitated. "I wanted to find Inez first. She works for Old Can Be Gold and may be mixed up in all this," she told him as Bess walked up. She had Nancy's jacket over her arm, too.

"If you're looking for Inez," Bess remarked, "don't bother. She cut out after she and Ethan had a heavy conversation. Ethan's still here, though. He seems to have suddenly developed an interest in George." Bess jerked her head over her shoulder.

Nancy saw George talking animatedly to Ethan. When George spotted Nancy, she headed directly for her, motioning Ethan to stay put.

"You're leaving?" George asked. "Look, I'm going to hang out here longer," she added, then lowered her voice. "Ethan's a wealth of information about Lou Knight and Carey Black. Anyway, if I wait until he can cut out of here, he said he'd show me something related to the tape. He's being pretty mysterious, but I thought I should follow through. He can drive me back to the condo afterward."

"Good idea," Nancy said. "The more information

we have about that tape and how this whole appraisal scene works, the better."

Clutching the mike, the blues singer wailed the closing bars to his song. He let the last note float over the audience gathered in the Back Street Blues Club.

The audience remained spellbound a second, then exploded into applause. Seated at a front corner table, Ned, Nancy, and Bess joined in enthusiastically.

"Ned, that was incredible!" Nancy exclaimed, clapping until her hands hurt. Before Ned could reply, the singer announced the next set would begin in forty-five minutes.

The singer came down the side steps of the small stage and walked toward Ned's table, holding out his hand. "Ned Nickerson?" he asked. Ned jumped up as the singer introduced himself. "Bobby Morgan. Greg's dad. Greg called earlier to make sure I'd reserve you a table."

"These are my friends Nancy Drew and Bess Marvin," Ned told the musician.

"We loved the show," Nancy told Mr. Morgan.

"That last song was awesome!" Bess added, her eyes still misty.

Bobby Morgan gave a little bow and beamed at the girls. "I thank you, but it seems you came because of some mysterious tape. Greg said you were pretty vague about it but needed me to listen to it?"

"If you can, Mr. Morgan," Nancy said. "A friend found it in her attic, and we want to know if it's authentic. Ned said you were an expert on some of the rock-blues crossover music of the late sixties and early seventies."

Bobby's dark eyes widened. "You've got *that* tape? The one with Lou Knight and Carey Black and Mama's Bad Boys?"

"You know about it?" Bess gasped.

Bobby Morgan chuckled. "I heard it turned up at an appraisal show. You bet I want to hear it. Come on, I've got a reel-to-reel set up in the back of the club." He led them backstage to a small but fully functional recording studio. A bank of recording equipment and a technical console were set up on the near side of a glass partition. Behind the partition was a microphone, with earphones draped across a music stand. A drum set was stashed in a far corner.

"So where's the tape?" Bobby said.

Ned took it out of his pocket. Before leaving the house Nancy had carefully slid it into a self-locking plastic bag. Ned handed Bobby the tape.

The musician looked at it with reverence. "You have no idea how many people have speculated about the existence of a tape of this jam session. Carey Black mentioned it in some interview, but the tape had vanished." As he spoke, Bobby unpacked the tape, flicked on his reel-to-reel player, then carefully threaded the lead in an empty spool. He spun some knobs, then looked up with his fingers crossed. "Here goes nothing," he said, his eyes bright with anticipation.

A blast of static was followed by the sound of a woman clearing her throat and the strum of an acoustic guitar. A deep, mellow female voice began to sing a traditional folk ballad. For a second Nancy was mesmerized by the hauntingly beautiful voice.

It was Ned who exclaimed, "That's not Lou Knight!"

Nancy snapped back to the present. "This isn't the tape we heard yesterday."

"But who's the singer?" Bess wondered.

"Me!" an angry voice cried from the door.

Nancy turned. "Lisa?" Lisa was standing in the doorway. Next to her were Ethan and George.

"Turn off that tape," Lisa demanded. Her dark eyes were furious. Her expression was a mixture of anger, shock, and hurt.

"This is *you?*" Bobby asked, switching off the music.

"Not that it's anyone's business," Lisa fumed, "but yes." Then, turning on Bess, she said through gritted teeth, "I can't believe you'd go snooping in my things when I wasn't around."

"Lisa, it wasn't like that," Bess answered. "I was looking for a scarf to wear to the party, and the tape was in your drawer."

"And you all just assumed that I had stolen the Lou Knight tape."

"Stolen?" Ethan looked aghast. "Did you know this earlier?" he asked George.

George looked embarrassed. "I couldn't tell you. It's part of an investigation."

"Into what?"

"Those burglaries," Lisa said sharply. "Jason knew about the tape and about Nancy's involvement in the burglary investigation."

Ethan shook his head. "Guess he was too busy tonight to mention it. He's with one of his model friends. They were heading out to an all-night club after the opening." To Nancy's dismay, Lisa proceeded to fill him in on all the details.

Meanwhile, Nancy took George aside. "What in the world are you doing here?"

"Bobby Morgan is a friend of Ethan's. Ethan wanted me to meet him to hear some bootlegged material that Bobby's collected over the years."

"But why is Lisa with you?" Bess wondered.

"Because she overheard him say we were going to the club, and she's a fan of Bobby's."

"You kids have really fallen into a pot of gold with that tape—too bad it's gone missing. I'll keep my eye out for it and notify the cops if copies turn up," Bobby promised.

Ethan stayed behind with Bobby, but Lisa left with Nancy and the others. Once they were outside, she said, "You guys owe me an apology, big time."

"Yes, we do, Lisa," Nancy said. "And I'm sorry. I've got no excuses except that the problem is how someone else would have had access to your apartment without your being involved. This tape rules you out." Nancy poked out her hand toward Lisa. "Friends?"

Lisa smiled wanly. "Yeah, I guess."

"How come I never knew you sang?" Bess asked.

"I just decided to give it a shot," Lisa said. "Now and then I perform at the smaller clubs. This tape is part of a demo I'm putting together."

"Well," Ned remarked, "with your voice you should have no problem finding a producer."

Lisa gave a bitter laugh. "Oh, it's about the same level of problem as Nancy is having finding the Old Can Be Gold thieves. Any luck?" she asked as they headed toward Nancy's car. Back Street Blues was within walking distance of Jason's loft, where Nancy had left the car parked.

"No. Do you have any new ideas?" Nancy asked. Lisa shrugged.

Nancy thought a minute. "The culprit has access

to Old Can Be Gold's database of clients and addresses. So the robberies have to be an inside job."

Lisa stopped in her tracks. "Do they?" she said, obviously puzzling something out in her mind. "I don't think so. I mean people can access anything over the Internet."

"Aren't Old Can Be Gold's records secure?" George wondered.

Ned laughed. "Nothing's totally secure online. And I doubt you'd need big-time hackers to break into Old Can Be Gold's files. I bet we could if we had access to a computer."

"We do—right down the block," Lisa said excitedly. "CyberScoops—it's an ice cream parlor/coffeehouse/Internet café. Come on. They're open all night!"

A few minutes later Nancy, George, Ned, and Bess were peering over Lisa's shoulder at a computer screen. The café was relatively empty so late on a Saturday night, but the coffee was good.

Nancy had her notebook open on her lap. At her suggestion, Lisa punched in the name of the couple in Denver, Max and Minnie Cordel. The search engine brought up several Cordels: a retail store, a cabaret singer named Max, a pet-food site, and finally something called Thriftytreasures.com.

"Let's try another name," Bess suggested, "and see if they have anything in common."

The next name they tried belonged to a woman in Memphis who'd had a small bronze Southeast Asian statue burgled. "L-A-P-P I-T-O." Lisa spelled out the name as she typed. The first four listings were for cheese and dairy products sold by a family in Wisconsin. But when Nancy spotted the fifth site, she grabbed Ned's arm. "Hey, there's Thriftytreasures again. We're onto something here," she said.

"Let's check it out." With a click of her mouse Lisa surfed over to Thriftytreasures.com. As the Web page loaded, Nancy looked on, amazed.

"This is no amateur site," she remarked. The Web page boasted a sophisticated design with colorful graphics. Reaching for the mouse, Nancy highlighted the first topic, "All About Us."

When the page downloaded, Nancy skimmed it quickly. "This is a sort of barter and bargain site," she said, vaguely disappointed. For a fee the site would connect potential sellers and buyers. Interesting, but it didn't seem to be a link to the robberies.

Lisa took the mouse back and went to the site's home page, where she clicked on something called "New and Of Note."

"Well, I'll be . . ." Lisa tapped a finger against the screen. "Look. Nancy, this is unbelievable! Quick, check your list."

Nancy looked at the screen and cried out, "Every single person that's been burgled is listed!"

"So Thriftytreasures is the—what?—the fence, the actual ring of thieves?" Ned wondered.

"I don't know. But we have to find out who's behind Thriftytreasures.com."

George drummed her fingers against the monitor, then spoke up. "Don't Web-based companies usually give their e-mail addresses?"

"Of course." Lisa scrolled to the bottom of the home page and read the e-mail address aloud. "Eyeriver@speedmail.com."

Lisa kept staring at the screen as if trying to puzzle something out. Suddenly she let out a soft moan. "Oh, Nancy, I know who this is!"

"Who?" Nancy demanded to know.

"I helped her pick it out when I first came to Old Can Be Gold. The whole crowd was at lunch one day trying to come up with cool screen names for one another. Mine was Songbird, and—"

"And," Nancy deduced, "Eyeriver is Inez Rivera!"

13

Double Exposure

Lisa dropped her hands to her lap and cried in dismay. "I refuse to believe Inez is involved in this scheme. And, anyway, how'd she pull off the burglaries? She's never been on the road with the show.

"Oh, Inez didn't personally commit the burglaries, Lisa. Believe me, the woman isn't working alone, I'm sure of that," Nancy declared, feeling vindicated. Her gut instincts had proved right once again. Inez had been acting vaguely suspicious and awfully nervous right from the get-go. "But the problem is proving all this. We've got part of the picture, but I can't connect the dots. Inez uses this Web site, but how? To notify the actual burglars where to hit next?"

For a moment everyone was silent. "Why don't we set her up?" Ned suggested.

"How?" George inquired.

Nancy shared a glance with Ned, then said, "We'll bait her with one of the objects appraised here at the show. One of us can pose as an interested buyer. I bet that within a couple of days that object is burgled, fenced, and offered to us."

"Not to *us*. To me," Ned volunteered. "Inez doesn't know me—at least not by name. I'll e-mail her now and check her reply tomorrow when I'm back at school. My ride's heading back to Emerson really early in the morning," he told Nancy.

Lisa pushed her chair over to make room for Ned in front of the keyboard.

"What is it I'd like to buy?" he asked.

"I know!" Bess cried gleefully. "That wooden Indian. That's a real guy sort of thing."

"Good idea," Nancy said. "But don't say you've seen it at Old Can Be Gold. Just that you collect cigar store Indian statues."

Once Ned had sent his e-mail, they left the café and dropped Ned off at his buddy's house. After he got out of the car, he poked his head back in the window. "Nancy, be careful," he urged. "If Inez knows you're onto her, she might warn the thieves." Ned hesitated. "Do you want me to hang out here tomorrow? I can grab a bus back to school tomorrow night."

"No, Ned. I'll be okay," Nancy promised, blowing him a kiss good night. "And don't forget to call me when Inez responds to your e-mail," she reminded him.

Back at Lisa's, Nancy was too psyched to sleep. In the wee hours she lay in bed, thinking about the case. Finding the Thriftytreasures.com site had really broken things open.

Inez wasn't working alone—and maybe, just maybe, she was somehow in league with Ethan. Like Jason, he had been on the road with the show. He really did seem amazed that the tape had been stolen, but Nancy was beginning to suspect that whoever stole the tape might not be behind the rest of the burglaries. Inez and Ethan were connected to each other, and possibly to the crimes.

Then there was Wes Clarke. Nancy wanted to scout out his premises before the show reopened its doors later in the day. Maybe she should snoop around Westfield's for any scrap of evidence to connect Ethan and Inez.

As for Jason, his pictures were either proof he was part of the crime ring, or they were simply copies of photos he had sent to clients.

Nancy dozed on and off until a faint early dawn light filtered through the guest room windows. In the next bed George was in a deep sleep, her breathing quiet and even. Moving very quietly, Nancy got up, grabbed her clothes, and carried them to the living room. There she dressed hurriedly in jeans, a sweatshirt, and sneakers, and tied her hair up in a ponytail. She started for the front door, then detoured to the kitchen, where she scrawled a hasty note: "I'm off early to the show to check something out. See you there later."

A few minutes later she was pulling out of the garage. Across the lake the gray sky was retreating before the first glimmer of sunrise. Traffic was almost nonexistent that early on a Sunday morning, and Nancy reached the sports complex in less than twenty minutes. She parked her Mustang at the far end of the lot.

To her surprise several cars were already parked in the employee parking area. Then two men approached the loading dock. One wore a security guard uniform, the other a windbreaker with the words Max's Hauling on the back. Nancy slipped behind the trailer of a truck and overheard them talking.

"Look, Will, I'm doing you a big favor here. I'm supposed to be at my post. The guys up top are nervous about a possible break-in."

What luck! Nancy realized. The entrance to the complex was temporarily unguarded as the men ducked into the trailer of a moving van. Nancy leaped onto the loading dock and in through the freight entrance.

She stopped at the open door to the gym to catch

her breath and to make sure she hadn't been followed. The gym was quiet. Probably only the one guard was on duty. Only a few security lights were lit, casting long mysterious shadows over the various appraisal booths, pieces of antique furniture, and statuary. The place felt positively haunted. Nancy decided to explore CrimeShoppers first.

When Nancy approached Wes's table, her heart sank. He had cleared off his display shelves and the surface of his table. He had probably stowed all his wares somewhere safe and secure—including the square box she had come to check out. Not really expecting to find anything, Nancy lifted the tablecloth. Beneath the table a stack of storage cartons formed a kind of shelf. And right on top of one of the cartons, was that familiar square box.

Nancy picked it up. It definitely was not the same box that George's tape had come in, but it *was* a reel-to-reel tape box. Carefully Nancy opened it and stared at its contents: Four neat stacks of mint-condition cards—the kind that came in bubble gum packs—were inside. Except these cards depicted famous criminals instead of sports stars. Nancy sat back on her heels and started to laugh.

Well, what did she expect? Wes *was* a crime memorabilia dealer. Nancy had heard of cards like these: gangster collector cards put out in the 1920s and '30s, when big-time crooks like Al Capone and Baby Face Nelson were pop icons.

Nancy's smile faded as she closed the box and carefully placed it exactly as she had found it, on top of the storage cartons. She got up, smoothed the wrinkles on the tablecloth, and shook her head. If Wes had taken the Lou Knight tape, he didn't have it here. And then there was still the matter of how that fingerprinting kit got into her bag. Nancy wasn't ready to dismiss Wes as a suspect either in the tape burglary or the bigger crime.

Nancy looked up: the windows high on the gym walls framed squares of pale blue sky. Nancy checked her watch. The sun was up, and she had no idea how early the Old Can Be Gold staff came to work.

Still hugging the shadows, she hurried across the room to Westfield's. The Westfield's site was larger and more elaborate than CrimeShoppers, with three glass-front display cases arranged as three sides of a square and serving as appraisal counters. Nancy stepped behind the makeshift counter, where there were a couple of tall chairs for the appraisers, some storage cartons, and plastic milk crates filled with files, catalogs, and some reference books. Pushing a chair out of her way, Nancy stooped down and riffled through the folders.

Most of the material was related to sales, bills of lading, and storage records. Suddenly her eye caught the name on one thick folder. It was printed in bold black felt-tip marker: "Ethan's Stash."

Nancy slipped the file out of the crate and opened it. There were notes about ceramic collectibles, the Arts and Crafts movement, Depression-era glass, and one legal-size yellow sheet of paper with an annotated list of music collectibles. Among the items most in demand by collectors were a Beatles autograph book worth several thousand dollars, posters from Grateful Dead concerts in the late 1960s or early '70s, and a guitar owned by Jimi Hendrix. Following the list of items was a list of names: possible collectors and/or possible sources of rare rock memorabilia.

There was nothing about the missing tape, but here was evidence enough that Ethan had connec tions to the music world beyond his friendship with Bobby Morgan. If Inez was involved in setting up robberies, then Ethan could easily provide a list of customers ready to pay big bucks for it.

And, of course, Ethan had access to records for all of Westfield's clientele. Between his connections and Inez's they barely needed professional fences, only goons to effect the actual break-ins.

Nancy wondered if she should take the list with her to check the names against the Thriftytreasures site or if she should just copy the names down in her notebook. Before she could decide, she heard the clicking of a woman's high heels. The footsteps were heading directly toward her.

Frantic, Nancy looked for a place to hide. Her eyes alighted on a big wardrobe. Staying low behind the counter, Nancy scurried toward the wardrobe and opened the door, praying it wouldn't creak. Fortunately its owner had been good about oiling the hinges. Nancy crept inside and closed the door, leaving it open just a crack for air. It was a tight fit, but she managed to scrunch herself in.

"Ethan Woodard, I owe you one!"

At the sound of Inez's voice, Nancy was barely able to stifle a gasp.

"You probably do," Ethan said. He sounded grumpy and sour. "What's going on that couldn't wait until later? I didn't get home until four this morning."

"That's not my fault. This is the only time we could hook up without anyone around," Inez snapped. "I told you at the party last night we needed to talk, but you wouldn't give me the time of day. You were too busy obsessing over that George—or is it her tape?"

Nancy heard Ethan emit a loud sigh. "Look, Inez, I know things ended badly between us last year, but get over it. And, yeah, that girl is nice, but she doesn't even live around here, and she's a little young for me. As for the tape," he added glumly, "someone stole it from Lisa's condo."

Inez gasped. "I didn't know that!" There was a

moment's silence. "That explains everything—why that friend of Lisa's is snooping around trying to find out about those burglaries."

"The burglaries?" Ethan suddenly sounded wary. "Inez, don't tell me you're involved—"

"No way!" Inez declared hotly, and Nancy smiled to herself. The girl sounded convincing. "But, Ethan, it's going to look like I'm chin deep in the whole mess." She paused, and when she continued, Nancy could hear she was on the verge of tears. "Everything that's been stolen has been listed on my Web site. Then, when I got home last night, there was a posting from a collector who wanted a particular kind of wooden Indian."

Ned's e-mail! Nancy realized, and pressed her ear against the crack in the door as Inez went on. "I know this sounds crazy, but there was something suspicious about it. There's an item like what he wants at the show, but the appraisal data and owner's address haven't even reached my desk yet. It's too much of a coincidence. Someone's going to tie me in with those burglaries, Ethan. Now, after that e-mail, I'm sure someone's onto my site—but for the wrong reasons! I'm no thief, and Thriftytreasures is just a smart business idea."

Nancy wished she could see Inez's face. Could she really be telling the truth?

"Inez." Ethan sounded grim. "I warned you

about starting Thriftytreasures. That was a crazy, greedy scheme, linking up collectors with potential sellers by using the Old Can Be Gold database."

"Maybe it is," Inez retorted. "But it's not illegal unless . . ." Nancy heard a note of suspicion enter Inez's voice. "You're the only person who knows about my connection to that site. How do I know you haven't used the base yourself for a whole scuzzy operation? And speaking of greed—you have no right to criticize me for being greedy. What about your brother? The guy's a money-hungry operator—where does his money come from?"

Ethan laughed tightly. "Look, I don't love seeing him rich, either, but he does earn those bucks. He works hard in a high-paying field. Take that fashion shoot he did last week. He's bragging that he bribed the doorman of a luxury condo on Lake Shore Drive to use an apartment for a shoot—just to impress Yvonne Bly. As you say, the guy's an operator—and greedy—" Ethan broke off. "Hey, you're not accusing Jason . . ."

"Maybe I am," Inez said. "Just think, he could have learned about my site from you."

"You think I'd tell him? I promised I wouldn't tell anyone about the site or your being behind it, Inez. *I* don't break promises," he added in an accusing tone.

"Why should I believe you?"

Ethan let out a bitter laugh. "You of all people

know I don't share very much with my brother. He is not my favorite person."

"Right," Inez scoffed. "I've heard that line before. You guys put on a big show of not liking each other, but I've always felt it's just an act."

"I can't believe I'm hearing this," Ethan fumed. "Especially from you. Jason is money hungry but no crook, and neither am I." Ethan suddenly cut himself off. "Someone's coming."

"Probably Security," Inez said with a calmness that amazed Nancy. "Don't worry. We're covered. I'm supposed to be here to accept an early-morning delivery of a museum-quality rolltop desk that Old Can Be Gold is moving to the show for the client."

"And my excuse?"

"You're with me."

Nancy listened as a security guard approached. He chatted briefly with Ethan and Inez, then left. A moment later Ethan and Inez headed off. Nancy waited a minute longer, then slipped out of the wardrobe, her head reeling.

What was it Ethan had said about Jason's renting a condo overlooking Lake Shore Drive for a fashion shoot? Nancy called to mind the photo on the wall at Jason's show. Of course it looked familiar. The view out the window in the photo was the same as the one from Lisa's terrace.

Nancy managed to slip past the security desk,

and a few moments later she was in her car, heading toward Jason's loft. When she arrived, Jason's street was deserted, the stores still closed. Nancy remembered noticing an alley running behind Jason's building and drove her Mustang into it, parking directly under the fire escape.

She got out of her car and closed the door softly. She looked up. "Yesss!" she exclaimed to herself. The window looking onto the third-floor fire escape was still open. Nancy nimbly climbed on top of the hood of her car and was just able to reach the first rung of the fire escape ladder. She grasped the iron bar, swung herself up, then began the climb to the third floor. She wasn't exactly sure how she'd deal with Jason, but she was pretty sure that at the very least he would still be asleep—and his bedroom was on the other side of the loft. If she was really lucky, Jason might still be out partying or maybe he had crashed with friends.

Nancy slipped through the window and gingerly eased herself over the sill. She stood very still, listening to hear if Jason was up or if anyone was moving about the loft. All she heard was silence. She let out her breath, then glanced around the studio. It was illuminated only by dim morning light coming through the north-facing windows. The photo she needed to look at was in the exhibit in the front part of the loft. Not knowing if Jason was home or not, she was afraid to risk venturing past his bedroom to get there. On the other hand, his darkroom was right off his office area. Like most photographers, Jason probably had more than one print of that model in the condo.

Nancy went to the darkroom, opened the door, and cringed as it squeaked on its hinges. She turned quickly and realized the study door was open—too late to close it now. She tiptoed into the darkroom. There were two or three stacks of prints on the counter, and a slew of negatives. Other prints were clipped to a line strung from one wall of the darkroom to the other. To see better, Nancy flicked on the safety light. Reaching up, she unclipped the two nearest black-and-white photos: they were of a curio cabinet filled with tribal art. Some photos were close-ups of particular items. One Nancy recognized instantly: the blow dart that had so intrigued George at Lisa's apartment.

"I don't believe this!" she muttered. Somehow Jason had gotten into Lisa's living room and photographed her aunt and uncle's collection.

After tucking the photos in her bag as evidence, Nancy turned to the stack of proofs beside the row of developing trays. The first two were simply overexposed copies of photos Jason had in his show. But the next group of pictures made Nancy want to shout for joy. Just as she suspected, the pictures were taken inside an apartment baring a strikingly similar layout to Lisa's, with the same beautiful view of skyline and lake in the distance.

"Gotcha!" Nancy murmured to herself, and then a familiar buzzing sound came from the depths of her purse. Nancy jumped, then remembered she had probably left her cell phone on. Nancy opened her bag and yanked out the phone.

"Nancy?" George's voice sounded worried and frightened. "Where are you?"

"You won't believe this," Nancy started to say, when suddenly she heard a sound behind her. As she turned, she was blinded by a flash of light. Then she heard something whoosh through the air above her, and finally something crashed down on her head.

Searing, hot pain exploded through Nancys brain. Her knees buckled, and someone grabbed the phone from her hand. She heard the sound of the phone snapping closed, breaking the connection with George.

A moan escaped Nancy's lips as she dropped to the floor. She fought to stay conscious in order to focus on her assailant. But as the shadowy figure loomed above her, the room dissolved into blackness and she passed out.

14

A Clever Ruse

As if from a great distance, Nancy heard a screech of brakes, then felt a sudden jolt. Her body jerked to one side, and her arm crashed against something hard and cold. As her eyes popped open, a wave of pain roared through her head. Her stomach clenched, and she fought back the urge to throw up. Closing her eyes again, she felt the nausea pass.

She touched her head and winced. She felt as if someone had taken her brain and used it as a bowling ball. Where am I? she wondered. Wherever she was, she was freezing. This time she opened her eyes slowly, and her surroundings gradually came into focus.

She was in some kind of train that was moving. A brief glance around and the daylight coming through the windows told her that she was on one of Chicago's elevated train lines. When the train's motion had jerked her awake, she had bashed her arm against the cold metal wall of the car.

"Hey, there's some kid in here!" someone shouted from the far end of the car. Nancy turned her head gingerly and saw a uniformed transit worker standing in the open door of the car. He motioned to someone in the next car, then strode up to Nancy. The man definitely looked annoyed, but as he neared, his expression changed.

"Are you okay?" he asked, his voice softening with concern.

"Yes. Yes," Nancy told him. "What line is this?"

"The Blue Line," he told her.

Nancy gasped as the memory of what happened flooded back to her. The Blue Line ran through Jason's neighborhood. "Look, I've got to get off this train!" Nancy said, jumping up. For a moment her legs felt as if they might give way, but Nancy grabbed the back of a seat and steadied herself. She realized that Jason had hit her on the head and then dumped her on this train. He wanted her out of his way, and all at once Nancy was sure she knew why. "I've got to get back downtown," she told the two men. "Where can I change trains?"

"Nowhere around here," the second man told her. "This train's going in for maintenance, and we're on a Sunday schedule, so it'll be a while. We're almost in the train yard. I guess Manny forgot to check this last car at the terminus. But you look like you've been hurt. I'm calling 911."

"No! What I need is to call a cab." Nancy reached for her bag and her cell phone. Then she saw her bag was missing. "My purse!" she cried.

"Look, I'm going to call the police," Manny said. "Obviously someone did something to you, ripped you off, and stashed you on this train."

Nancy put a hand over the Manny's walkie-talkie. "I promise to call the police. I know who did this. First I've got to get back to town. Couldn't you just call me a cab and lend me the fare?"

The men looked dubious, but at Nancy's insistence they broke down. Using his own cell phone, Manny called a local cab company, telling them to pick up Nancy at the train-yard office. Nancy borrowed his phone to call Lisa's house but only got the machine. Everyone was probably at Old Can Be Gold. Or, she realized with a pang of guilt, out looking for her. How had George reacted when Nancy answered her cell phone, and then not said a word—or had she? Nancy couldn't remember the moments just before Jason attacked her.

Fifteen minutes later, after taking Manny's address to send him a check to repay him, Nancy was on her way back to town. As she rode back in the cab, she was furious with herself, and with Jason. What a two-faced creep! A two-faced *smart* creep. The guy had a really good scheme going for him, and unless Nancy could get back to the condo and into the apartment next to Lisa's before Jason did, he'd erase all evidence of his crime. He only had to destroy his negatives, then move his equipment out of the condo, and he could claim to know nothing. The doorman and the super would play dumb.

Nancy barely waited for the cab to come to a full stop in front of Lisa's building before jumping out.

The doorman was the one from the day shift, not Carl. He recognized Nancy, who smiled but continued straight for the elevator. Fortunately, she didn't need a key to Lisa's apartment. When the elevator opened on the twentieth floor, Nancy punched in Lisa's door code and entered the apartment.

No one was home. She headed right for the terrace. Stepping outside, she shivered in the stiff cold breeze blowing off the lake.

Nancy climbed over the cast-iron divider onto the next terrace. Pressing herself against the narrow strip of brick wall, she hazarded a glance through the glass doors. Now, by daylight, she could see the room was filled with photo equipment, but the lights were out and it looked deserted. That surprised her. Jason should have headed right to the condo to clear out his stuff the minute he had gotten rid of Nancy and before she had a chance to call the cops.

Why hadn't he? The doorman! Carl was off until four, and the super didn't cover the door until around twelve. If Jason had paid Carl and the super to let him use the apartment for the shoot, he wouldn't risk the other doorman not letting him in the building. Jason would wait until the super covered for the daytime doorman.

Nancy checked her watch. It was almost noon, the time the doorman broke for lunch. That left her about fifteen minutes. The terrace door was still locked, but the lock, like Lisa's, was easy to jimmy. Then Nancy's stomach sank. Without her purse and wallet she didn't have a credit card or even the little picklock set she always carried along with her penknife. The penknife! Before climbing Jason's fire escape, Nancy had taken it out of her bag and stuffed it in her pocket just to have it handy.

She reached into the back pocket of her jeans. The knife was still there. Nancy opened it and slipped the blade between the doorframe and the door. On the first try she pried it open and let herself in.

Nancy's gaze swept the apartment. Jason had certainly camouflaged his activities. The place was still partially set up for a fashion shoot, with standing tungsten lamps and an old-fashioned sofa set up in front of a cloth backdrop. Yvonne Bly's black cocktail outfit was hanging on a garment rack, together with a couple of men's tuxedos and some fancy silk ties. The whole thing looked totally legit, except perhaps for Jason's unusual rental arrangement with the building staff. Even that was not high crime, not a big deal—but assault and burglary were.

Nancy quickly searched the apartment, but the bedrooms were bare, the closets empty. She went back into the living room, disappointed, and started toward the terrace door. She noticed that the drapery behind the sofa was bulging slightly.

She lifted the creamy fabric and hit pay dirt. Sure enough, George's battered reel-to-reel tape recorder was there, but was the tape still inside?

Hopeful, Nancy opened the lid. Two reels of tape were set up to play, with the leader already threaded in the empty spool. Nancy unplugged one of the lights from an extension cord and plugged in the tape recorder. The On button lit up. She pressed Play and sat back on her heels. There was static, some voices, and then Lou Knight and Carey Black jamming what became Mama's Bad Boys' last hit song.

At the end of the song Nancy turned the tape off. When she reached for Rewind, she accidentally pushed Fast Forward. Just as she punched the Off button, a voice exclaimed from behind her, "Girl, you sure have one hard head!"

15

Over the Edge

"Jason?" Nancy recognized the voice.

He didn't answer. "Now get up—slowly!" he commanded, prodding Nancy in the back with some kind of hard object.

A gun? Nancy's heart leaped to her throat. She started to turn.

"Don't turn around!" he snarled. He prodded her again, pushing her slightly forward. Nancy's hand was on the tape recorder. Thinking quickly, she pressed the Record button. "Get up! Now!"

"Okay, okay!" Nancy got up slowly, keeping her eyes focused on the glass of the terrace door. It was clean and shiny, and Nancy could see Jason's reflection perfectly. "Jason, you're only making things worse for yourself."

Jason's lips curled into a self-satisfied smile. "Don't you get it? I'm not Jason."

Nancy's jaw dropped, and she started to turn to see for herself.

"No looking. That'd be cheating," he said.

As he talked, Nancy felt the pressure against her back let up. Maybe if she could distract him, she could make a break for it. The terrace door was still half open.

"You know what happened this morning or you wouldn't be here," she said. "Jason must have told you. I searched his darkroom and came up with clear evidence that he had a shoot here."

"Really, that's pretty lame evidence," Ethan sneered.

A sliver of doubt entered Nancy's mind. Was this really Ethan? Bess had blabbed to Jason, but who else knew Nancy was on the case? Then she remembered overhearing Inez tell Ethan.

Nancy ignored his jibe and continued her story. "He bribed building staff to let him use this condo for a shoot—but only because it was next door to Lisa's aunt and uncle's art collection."

"Creative thinking, but no way to prove that."

"Wrong!" Nancy went on. "I saw photos of the collection in Jason's darkroom."

Nancy saw a sudden movement reflected in the terrace door. Someone else had come through the front door. It was another man. Nancy's heart sank. If this was Ethan's accomplice, she was in big trouble. She had a chance at subduing one man, but two at once . . .

"Jason!" the other man exclaimed. "Are you crazy?"

Whichever twin was behind Nancy spun around. Nancy sprang to the side, darting out of reach. She made it as far as the terrace door before she noticed it was Jason who had just arrived. Or was it Ethan? They weren't dressed alike, but their faces were identical. The twin who'd held her captive was wearing nylon warm-up pants and a matching anorak. Some kind of black cloth was draped over his right hand, concealing the hard object he'd shoved in Nancy's back. The guy at the door was dressed for work in a sports jacket, a turtleneck, and dark brown pants.

One of these guys was Ethan. Nancy had heard Ethan earlier at the Old Can Be Gold site, but she hadn't gotten even a glimpse of his shoes.

"Is that a gun?" the newcomer asked, stunned.

"Of course not!" The first twin tossed aside the cloth to reveal a small collapsible tripod. As he did, Nancy noticed his watch—a Rolex. It *had* been Jason all along holding her captive. "So how'd you find me here, *Jason*?" he asked, positioning himself between Nancy and the terrace door.

Ethan frowned. "Jason, stop playing this twin game. What's going on here? Have you lost it?"

"You can cut the act. Nancy is probably wise to us now."

"To *us*?" Ethan gasped. He closed the front door behind him and walked down the steps from the foyer into the living room. He was staring in horror at his brother.

"Tell her why you're here, then," Jason said, folding his arms across his chest and jerking his head toward Nancy.

"You weren't at the loft this morning. You wanted more information about that tape, and I didn't have a chance to tell you last night—it's been stolen," Ethan said. Then to Nancy's horror his eyes lit on the open tape recorder.

Nancy saw Ethan's expression register total shock as he realized it was recording. She cringed, waiting for him to say something to Jason. "Oh, you have the recorder," he said, then managed to tilt the lid so the revolving tape was hidden from Jason's view. Ethan avoided glancing at Nancy. He was aware the tape was recording what could be devastating evidence against himself and his brother. And he let it keep playing.

Nancy couldn't believe it. Maybe Ethan was innocent.

"Yeah, I got that tape. It's pretty cool," Jason said. "We can share in this big-time, bro! With your connections this tape is going to set us up for life."

"We? Us? Hey, keep me out of this. Look, I know you stole the tape. How you knew about it before you rented this apartment is beyond me."

"I didn't." Jason shrugged. "I overheard Lisa talking about her aunt's collection. I have clients interested in tribal art, and by the way, I found them on your girlfriend's Web site."

"Thriftytreasures?" Ethan exclaimed.

"Don't look so shocked. Once I find a buyer on the black market, my associates obtain the goods."

"Thieves, not associates!" Nancy corrected angrily. "So you are behind the burglaries," she accused, knowing that the tape was still recording.

"I play my part. I get my cut," Jason bragged. "A big one—believe me."

"But what about the tape? How does the tape fit in?" Nancy prodded, wanting to get the whole story recorded.

Jason leaned against the sofa and actually looked proud. "Before I made my move on Lisa's apartment, you girls and that tape turned up. You left it right in the middle of the living room—or practically in the middle of the living room—and Lisa never locks that terrace door. Hey"—he lifted his shoulders and flashed a charming smile—"it was mine for the taking. I put the tribal stuff on hold. It'll keep."

"So that's where your money comes from." Ethan sounded disgusted.

"Yeah, and if you stop with the good-guy act, you'll get your share, too—that is, if you don't have some kind of in already." Jason snickered. "You know, from Inez and her cute little side business."

"Inez is no thief, and she hasn't stolen a thing."

"Maybe, maybe not. But she is the perfect fall guy. The cops will be looking at Thriftytreasures pretty closely, and once we get rid of this snoop—"

"We?" Ethan paled, then grit his teeth. "You're a jerk, Jason. I'm not a thief, and I'm not getting rid of anyone." He paused, then tackled his brother, shouting, "Except you!"

Taken totally off guard, Jason fell, hard. Ethan threw his body on top of Jason, trying to pin him to the ground. Nancy sprang away from the window to help Ethan. She looked for something to use as a weapon. She reached for a lamp on the table by the sofa, but Jason's fingers reached it first. He yanked it out of Nancy's grasp and managed to bring it down on Ethan's head.

Ethan groaned and rolled off Jason. Disoriented, he tried to struggle to his feet, but Jason was quicker. Like a cat he jumped up and kicked his brother hard.

Frantic, Nancy grabbed the tripod, brandishing it at Jason as he plunged toward her. "You'll be sorry for this!" he roared, expertly maneuvering out of her grasp. Reaching for her right arm, he wrenched it behind her back, twisting her wrist until she dropped the tripod. He started pulling her toward the terrace.

"Little snoop was out on the balcony on a windy day, and she tripped and fell!" he said, struggling to drag her toward the railing.

Nancy managed to free one arm as Jason pressed her back against the railing. She felt him try to pick her up. Nancy planted her feet and with her last bit of strength aimed a karate kick at Jason's head. She made contact, hard.

He yowled and fell backward, slamming his head against the concrete floor of the terrace. He lay, writhing in pain, as Nancy steadied herself against the railing, trying not to look twenty stories down.

At the same instant the door to Lisa's terrace flew open, and two police officers swarmed over the divider, racing to Nancy's rescue.

George was right behind the cops, and so was Bess. Nancy was trying to catch her breath, but as she caught George's eye, she managed a wry grin. "Hey," she said, gesturing toward the apartment. "I found the tape. It's inside, but it might have a problem."

"Wonder what your aunt Betty and uncle Nick would think of this party?" Nancy murmured to Lisa that evening, in the living room of Lisa's condo. Open boxes of pizza and jugs of soda were arranged on the coffee table.

"Aunt Betty would say this is an eclectic crowd." Lisa hazarded a nervous smile. "And it's not exactly my idea of a party," she said, making a face.

"Mine either. And your aunt would definitely not be happy about the occasion," Bess commented.

All four girls were seated on the floor in front of the coffee table. On a long side table by the bookcase was a tape recorder. Bobby Morgan and Ethan Woodard were hovering over it.

"I just hope she doesn't make me move out," Lisa said ruefully.

"She won't," George predicted, grabbing a piece of pizza and popping rounds of pepperoni into her mouth. "Now more than ever she's going to want an apartment sitter."

"But one who locks terraces!" Mr. Landowski teased, patting Lisa on the shoulder. He pulled up a chair and poured himself some seltzer. "None of this is your fault, Lisa. Right, Carson?"

Nancy looked up at her dad. As soon as Nancy phoned him, he had driven from River Heights to advise George in case there were legal questions about ownership of the tape.

"Eddie's absolutely right," Carson reassured Lisa. "This was a very sophisticated professional operation. I wouldn't be surprised if the investigation leads to a pretty high-powered art theft ring. Jason's actually small-time here."

"He still caused some pretty big trouble," Nancy said, her back still smarting from her struggle with Jason earlier. The cops had arrested him, designated the vacant apartment as a crime scene, and brought everyone—including Nancy, George, Lisa and Bess—in for questioning.

Inez was cleared of any wrongdoing, but Mr. Landowski was furious with her and had fired her on the spot. He was threatening to sue her over her Thriftytreasures site. At the very least, Nancy had to agree that the venture had been unethical. But Ethan was going to bat for her, trying to ward off any legal action.

As for the tape, it took Carson, an entertainment lawyer representing Lou Knight's estate, and Eddie Landowski to convince the cops to give it up—at least for the evening. They needed to hold the tape until Jason's trial because Nancy had recorded Jason's conversation.

Ethan had objected strongly—the tape was possibly a very valuable property, and a copy should be made immediately of Lou Knight's song . . . unless Nancy had recorded Jason's voice over it.

While they had waited for the detectives from the local precinct to bring the tape back, the lawyer said that the legal issues of ownership were complicated, but in any event George would receive some hefty compensation whether it was sold at auction, bought by a recording company, or claimed by Lou Knight's heirs.

Bobby turned from the sideboard and called the room to attention. "Well, here goes nothing," he said, winking at Nancy.

As Bobby pressed Play, Nancy crossed her fingers. He'd transferred the tape to a modern reel-to-reel machine. That in turn was hooked up for dubbing on another reel-to-reel studio-quality machine.

Static erupted from the speakers. The sound fidelity was ten times truer than on the old battered machine. There was the sound of voices, some laughter, and then a deep male voice counting "And one . . . and two . . . and . . ." The room filled with the gritty unproduced version of Lou Knight's trademark tune, Knight's voice blending with Carey Black's. The song ended, and one of the detectives motioned for Bobby to turn off the tape before Jason's voice could come on. Nancy's body sagged with relief. She hadn't erased the important part of the tape.

When Bobby looked up, his eyes glittered with tears. "Now, that is something I never thought I'd hear . . . not in this lifetime." He turned to George and grinned. "You've got yourself the gen-u-ine article: Lou Knight's lost last song!"

American S·I·S·T·E·R·S

Join different sets of sisters as they embark on the varied, sometimes dangerous, always exciting journeys across America's landscape!

West Along the Wagon Road, 1852

A *Titanic* Journey Across the Sea, 1912

Voyage to a Free Land, 1630

Adventure on the Wilderness Road, 1775

Crossing the Colorado Rockies, 1864

Down the Rio Grande, 1829

Horseback on the Boston Post Road, 1704

Exploring the Chicago World's Fair, 1893

Pacific Odyssey to California, 1905

by Laurie Lawlor

A MINSTREL® BOOK

Published by Pocket Books

2200-05